Richard Rowlatt

Entranced with a dream

A Novel. Vol. 2

Richard Rowlatt

Entranced with a dream
A Novel. Vol. 2

ISBN/EAN: 9783337046248

Printed in Europe, USA, Canada, Australia, Japan

Cover: Foto ©Andreas Hilbeck / pixelio.de

More available books at **www.hansebooks.com**

ENTRANCED WITH A DREAM.

A NOVEL.

BY

RICHARD ROWLATT,

AUTHOR OF 'FISHING IN DEEP WATERS.'

IN THREE VOLUMES.

VOL. II.

LONDON: F. V. WHITE & CO.,
31 SOUTHAMPTON STREET, STRAND, W.C.

1883.

COLSTON AND SON, PRINTERS, EDINBURGH.

ENTRANCED WITH A DREAM.

CHAPTER I.

THE telegram had not arrived at Elston Court when Sir Edward Harewood dismounted from his horse in the presence of Mr Cresswell, who was at the door ready to receive him.

After a few words had passed between them, Mr Cresswell said,—

'When we made our arrangements last evening respecting the telegram, I forgot that the answer arriving here directed to me might raise the curiosity of my wife and daughter, and lead to unpleasant questions. To avoid which I gave your name as the person to whom the answer was to be sent. Had the idea occurred to me before I left you, I should have **sought** your permission first.'

'Then I am glad it did not occur **to you,'** rejoined Sir Edward, 'as I could **only have** looked upon it as a piece of needless formality.'

'Should it reach you,' said Mr **Cresswell,** 'in the presence of my wife and Edith, **you** will, if you please, treat it as a private **matter.'**

A smiling welcome awaited Sir Edward **at** the door of the dining-room. The mother **and** daughter, without knowledge of the **reason,** were fully alive to the fact that Mr **Cresswell** had been impatiently awaiting the coming **of** his friend, which, on his appearance, **added** to the pleasure they always derived from **his** visits.

While the breakfast was in progress, **the** expected telegram was placed in Sir **Edward's** hand.

'For me?' he said, as the servant **presented** it to him. 'Will you permit me,' he **added to** Mrs Cresswell, as he prepared to open it. **'Oh,** I see,' he murmured, half aloud. 'Yes, it **shall** be attended to. No answer at present,' **he said** to the man, who was waiting at the door. **' It** is curious to observe,' he continued, as he **put** the paper into his pocket, 'the changes **that** are insensibly stealing over us. It is **but a** very few years since, when such a missive as this made its appearance at the door of a house, every one within was thrown into a painful state of excitement. Now, on the contrary, it is looked upon quite as a matter of course, and creates little more curiosity than a letter.'

'I think you rather overrate your case,' observed Edith. 'A telegram is perhaps in a fair way of becoming the common thing you have described; but surely it has not reached that point yet.'

'I shall hold to my statement that it has,' replied Sir Edward, 'unless you can produce some proof to the contrary.'

'I can only answer for myself,' replied Edith, 'and I must confess I should receive twenty letters with less emotion than one solitary telegram.'

'But, my love,' observed Mrs Cresswell, 'that may arise from the fact of your having so few of them.'

'I am told,' said Mr Cresswell, 'that in the great business houses in London nothing is more common than for them to be sent out by dozens, and others received in the same way, with less notice than would formerly have been given to the despatch or arrival of a double letter.'

'And not much before my time,' observed Sir Edward.

'I will not attempt,' said Edith, 'to tax my memory with any such thing as a double letter or a member's frank. I am content to own I have heard of them.'

'Your two boys will come over to luncheon, I trust,' observed Mr Cresswell.

'Yes,' replied Sir Edward; 'they were greatly flattered with your invitation, and promised to come early.'

'I think,' observed Edith, 'that Oliver is looking better and stronger than he did a few months since.'

'Poor boy,' said Sir Edward, 'he has been the great trial of my life. His sad, shy, and dreamy manner has at times taxed my patience very severely; but I agree with you, he appears stronger than he did.'

In this way the hour of breakfast passed. A suspicion of the real object of Sir Edward's visit did not enter the minds of either of the ladies. They understood that it related to some private affair which need not excite their curiosity.

The breakfast over, the gentlemen retired to the library, and there, in a short time, their resolution was formed and acted upon with respect to the business in hand. By the telegram it appeared that there could be no doubt about the projected tour by a party of gentlemen, though, in consequence of the arrangements not yet being completed, no names were sent.

'You decide, then,' said Sir Edward, 'to let him draw upon you for the sum required?'

'Yes,' replied Mr Cresswell; 'it seems the only way I can free myself from his importunities, and if it must be so, I can have no wish to lengthen out the very unpleasant business.'

'And you will write to him?' said Sir Edward.

'No, I think not,' replied Mr Cresswell. 'I will send the order to my friend, and beg him to let him have it. That will give me a little quiet, I trust, from a troublesome and vexatious correspondence.'

'I trust it may.'

'But you are doubtful?'

'I must confess,' replied Sir Edward, 'that I am not a little so.'

'You would have me leave his application unnoticed?'

'Yes; or I would desire him to do just as he pleased about coming to England, but that nothing he could say would induce me to make him a more liberal allowance than he is now in receipt of, though it might occasion the loss of that.'

'I can only repeat,' replied Mr Cresswell, 'what I said last night—that if I alone were concerned I would act in a very different manner. But it is useless to talk or vex one's self more upon the subject; so, if you please, we will for the present dismiss it from our minds, and rejoin the ladies'— a proposition that Sir Edward was most willing to agree to, as any conversation in connection with the name of his false friend was very disagreeable to him.

Ere the luncheon was on the table, Oliver and Jesse drew rein at the door of the Court, and were soon in the presence of the occupants of the drawing-room.

The usual greeting over, Oliver, at his brother's request, opened the subject of the accident that had happened to Philip. Before he had proceeded far with his narrative, he was stopped by his father asking nervously how many of the party carried guns.

'All of us,' replied Oliver, 'except Jasper— that is, Jesse and myself, with Smith and Dixon.'

'And was not Philip with you?' asked Sir Edward.

'No; we saw nothing of him till after the accident; but Smith told us when we met him that Philip had given him to understand that he was tired of his employment, and meant to set off for London directly.'

'And if he had held to his purpose,' observed Jesse, 'he must have been far away by the time we heard of his going.'

'But he is not gone?' questioned Sir Edward.

'No; as I was just about to tell you, we found him by the side of the wood severely wounded.'

'Do you mean me to understand that the youth is dead?'

'He was not when we reached him,' said Jesse, 'and so as soon as we could we summoned Mr Saddler to our assistance, and, at his request, the coachman put the horses to the brake and took him to the hospital.'

'And who went with him?'

'His father,' replied Jesse; 'and I almost forgot to say,' he added, 'that he begged me to explain to you the cause of his going if you should return home and want him before he could be back.'

'This is a sad account you have brought us,' said Mr Cresswell.

'You have not told us how you discovered him, or the nature of the accident,' said Sir Edward.

'Did you not understand Oliver to say he was shot?'

'Shot!—and by whom?' asked Sir Edward.

'We think,' replied Jesse, 'that his gun went off by accident. Our attention was called to him by the cries of his father.'

'His father!' repeated Sir Edward. 'How came he there?'

'We cannot tell,' replied Jesse; 'but in answer to his cries, we hurried in the direction from whence they appeared to come, and there amongst the bushes by the side of the wood we found Philip stretched on the ground, with his father on his knees by his side, endeavouring to staunch the flow of blood from a gunshot wound in his neck.'

'Poor fellow!' said Sir Edward. 'It seems strange that, notwithstanding the disobedience and ingratitude of his son, he should be so greatly attached to him. Did he tell you how it happened that he was there?'

'No,' replied Jesse; 'and it did not occur to me to ask him.'

'There seems something very strange about the whole affair, according to your report. Is he not the same youth who gave you so much trouble by his leaving his father and going to London some time since ?' inquired Mr Cresswell.

'The same, I am sorry to say,' replied Sir Edward.

'And were you there and saw all that took place ?' asked Edith of Oliver.

'Yes, I was there,' replied Oliver, with a quivering voice—'that is, I was at a little distance. They did not want me near him.'

'But you made yourself very useful,' said Jesse. 'You ran for the doctor, and when you had secured his services, you went to the stables for the brake.'

Sir Edward looked pityingly at his first-born, but he made no marked observation on his conduct.

'Do you not think,' he said to Mr Cresswell, 'that I ought immediately to return home ?'

'No, I do not,' replied Mr Cresswell. 'If the wounded man had been left with uncertain and unskilful attendance, there might be reason for your doing so, but as it is, the case is very different, and I shall hold you to your promise to spend the day with us.'

Sir Edward saw the reasonableness of this, yet his anxiety was so great to get home that he

left Elston Court an hour or two earlier than
he otherwise might have done.

Oliver, of his own will, never put his pony to
its full speed, and he had on more than one
occasion expressed his annoyance to his brother
when he had urged him to do so, but there
was no escape for him from a hard gallop
on this return journey by the side of his
father.

On reaching home, Sir Edward could learn
little more of the accident than he already
knew. The father of the wounded youth had
not yet returned from the hospital, and the
grandfather professed to be quite ignorant of
the movements of his grandson.

'But I am told he was here with you a short
time before the accident occurred,' observed Sir
Edward.

'Only for a few minutes, Sir Edward.'

'Did he say anything to you of his going to
London ?'

'I think he did, but I can't remember what it
was. My memory is very bad to-day, and the
accident has quite upset me, and I am a little
deaf; and he talks so fast, and always about
some nonsense or other, that I should scarcely
know all he said if I could hear and remember
as well as I used to do.'

The questioning to which Smith was subjected appeared but little more satisfactory.

'You have told me,' said Sir Edward, 'that the youth left you two hours before the accident occurred. Had he his gun with him then?'

'I did not see it, Sir Edward.'

'But if you saw him leave the house, you surely must know whether he had it or not.'

'I only saw a small bundle in his hand, but I did not pay much attention to him. He appeared to be in an ill humour, and I thought the less I said to him the better.'

'Why so?'

'Because, Sir Edward, I know he could use his tongue very freely, and I did not want to have any words with him.'

'He has not been on very friendly terms with any of you, I am afraid. Who did you say were out with you yesterday?'

'Mr Oliver, Mr Jesse, with Dixon and Jasper.'

'No one else?'

'No, Sir Edward, my other assistants were at a good distance from us.'

'You are quite certain of that?'

'Quite, Sir Edward.'

'And those you have named were generally in your sight.'

'Yes, Sir Edward, though we were sometimes hidden from one another by the trees
and bushes.'

'You all had guns?'

'Yes, excepting Jasper.'

'I do not know why I should not be content
with what you have told me, but I should like
to ask you if your apparent dislike to each
other has ever led to an open quarrel?'

'No,' replied Smith; 'but his manner has
often been very provoking,—even Mr Jesse has
noticed it.'

'Mr Jesse, did you say?'

'Yes, Sir Edward, only two days since, and
I think he said he had spoken to you about him.'

'Did you discover if the gun found by the
side of the wounded youth had been lately
discharged?'

'It had every appearance of it, Sir Edward.'

'And you can form no idea of why the youth
was at that time there?'

'No, Sir Edward, unless what he said to me
about his going was only made up for his own
amusement, and that he intended to come out
and surprise us.'

'He knew you would be there?'

'Yes, I told him before he spoke about his
going to London.'

After Smith had left the library, Sir Edward sat for some time musing upon the unpleasant subject that had so suddenly come before him. Gradually, his thoughts became more serious and distressing. It was but as a shadow that the idea first crossed his mind, that the true account of the so-called accident had not yet reached his ear. Smith's saying recurred to his mind, that Philip had at times been very provoking, and that even Mr Jesse had noticed it. That he could well believe, as his son had spoken to him more than once upon the subject, and had wished him to find some employment for him amongst strangers, as he did not appear to value the society of his friends.

Was it possible that a quarrel had taken place amongst them, and that the shot had been fired by other hands than by those of the wounded youth? He knew Jesse was quick and impetuous, and that he could ill brook the empty pretentions of any one, and especially those of the conceited Philip; but he had too much confidence in the rectitude of his mind to think for a moment that he could be guilty of a premeditated crime, but what he might have done on the impulse of sudden anger, was not so easy to determine. 'Can it be,' he thought, 'that something of what I fear has taken place, and the story of the accident, with all its strangeness, has been brought to me to conceal a fearful crime?'

'I will not think of it,' he murmured, as he rose from his chair and walked nervously up and down the room. 'The supposition is too horrible. I must wait until Lea's return for the solution of the mystery. At present I dare not, even in thought, pursue the subject further.'

But that night the man, for whom he was so anxiously waiting, did not return. In the couse of the evening the coachman drove into the stable yard, and, in answer to a question from his master, said, 'I waited, Sir Edward, some time for him, but I only saw him just before I left, and then he was so put out that he could scarcely speak to me. He said his son was very bad, and he hoped you would excuse him for not coming back with me. The doctor,' he said, 'had given him permission to remain in the hospital, as the case was a very serious one, and he might perhaps be wanted in the night.'

The next morning Sir Edward was early at the keeper's house, unrefreshed and full of serious doubts. During the night he had earnestly striven to drive them away, but in vain. Sleeping or waking they would be present with him. He knew that if the injury to the wounded man should prove fatal, a strict inquiry into every circumstance of the miserable affair would be gone into. The fact that he had been on unfriendly terms with all around him, and if, as his fears suggested, the report should get abroad that he had died by other hands than his own, what could he say to stop the idle talk that would be indulged in? Nothing—simply nothing.

The inquiry must go on, whatever it might lead to; all that he could do was without loss of time to make himself acquainted with the whole affair in all its bearings, as far as he was able. With this view, he was on his way to Smith to question him still more closely than he had yet done.

Disappointment, however, awaited him at the end of his little journey. The keeper, he learnt, was out on his rounds, and Mrs Smith had taken her sick child to see the doctor. He had met the other children on their way to school; but so absorbed had he been in his own thoughts that he did not even see them, though they had done their best to gain his attention by their curtsies, smiles and bows.

Miss Montag and the maid were the only persons in the house, and Sir Edward having discovered the fact, was about to turn from the door, when the thought struck him that perhaps he might learn something from them, which would help to clear up his doubts. Since Lady Harewood's death, although he had had but little personal communication with Miss Montag, he had been very careful to perform the duties he had then undertaken. He had sent her to a good school, besides arousing Mrs Gibson's warmest sympathies in her behalf, so that he might be assured that she was not growing up in a state of useless ignorance, and the result had justified his care. She was now, he saw, on the threshold of womanhood, and would soon be fit to undertake the further duties he had marked out for her as a farmer's wife.

But as his purpose was thus far entirely un-known to the young lady herself, it could not in any manner have contributed to her rejection of Philip Lea, or create any nervousness re-specting it when she was addressed by her patron. The occurrence of yesterday had given her a great fright, from which she had now by no means perfectly recovered. The fear upper-most in her mind, after she heard that Philip had been shot, was that he had told some one of what had passed between them, and that it would be said she had driven him to commit suicide.

She was sorry to hear of his misfortune ; but she dreaded, above all things, to have her name mentioned in any way in connection with his.

Accustomed as Sir Edward was to call upon Smith, he created no undue excitement in the minds of the young people he found in the house. After hesitating for a few moments at the door, he said,—

' I think I will come in and wait for Mrs Smith's return. You say you expect her back very soon.'

' Yes ; very soon, Sir Edward,' replied Miss Montag, as she placed a chair for him and motioned to the maid, who stood with open mouth in the doorway that led to the kitchen.

Sir Edward saw the movement, and said,—

' No, no, let her remain here ; I may have occasion to speak to her.'

Miss Montag blushed scarlet, but she did not reply, while the maid, pulling down her sleeves and smoothing her hair, advanced a step or two further into the room.

' Perhaps you can give me,' said Sir Edward, ' some account of the sad accident that happened so near to you yesterday.'

' I am afraid we cannot tell you anything new,' replied Miss Montag. ' Mr Smith said he had spoken to you about it, and we know nothing more than he has told us.'

'Have any of the other men been here this morning?'

'I have not seen any,' replied Miss Montag.

'Yes, miss,' broke in the maid, 'Dixon was here before master went out.'

'And did he tell you anything?'

'He told me at the back door that it was a bad job for Philip, and that he was awful sorry, but that he couldn't make it out at all.'

'Not make what out?' asked Sir Edward.

'How he came to shoot himself there,' said the maid.

'Did he say he shot himself?'

'Yes, Sir Edward, and—'

'But he did not tell you so,' interposed Miss Montag.

'Yes, he did, miss, and more than that, he said he shouldn't wonder if he did it a purpose, he was such a queer fellow.'

'You are talking nonsense,' said Miss Montag.

'Well, miss, if I am, I am only saying what he said.'

'Then, I suppose,' said Sir Edward, 'he did not like him?'

'No, I don't think he did, that I don't.'

'Sir Edward does not wish to hear what you think.'

' Just let her tell me why she thinks so,' said Sir Edward.

'You see,' said the maid, 'when they are out by the back door, I often hear the men talking together, and once I heard Dixon and Philip talking very loud.'

' Quarrelling, you mean ? '

' Yes, and I heard them say something about knocking somebody down.'

' But there was no fighting ?' interposed Miss Montag.

'No,' said the maid ; 'I think they were both afraid to begin.'

' Thank you, that will do,' said Sir Edward ; ' I will not keep you any longer from your work.'

It was no small relief to Miss Montag when she saw the door close upon the girl. She had been upon thorns the whole time she was speaking, in momentary expectation that she would blurt out something respecting the manner in which Philip behaved in the house. Happily the girl's thoughts had not tended in that direction, and very earnestly Miss Montag hoped they never would.

But now she was brought face to face with

her great fear. How could she answer her patron, when he observed,—

'Your little maid appears to be well acquainted with what has passed at the back of the house, may I expect the same from you of the front?'

After a slight hesitation, she replied,—

'Perhaps I am not so much interested in listening to the conversation of the men as she is. I do not myself remember having heard any word passing between them that particularly arrested my attention.'

At this point Mrs Smith returned from her visit to the doctor. On her entrance, Sir Edward said,—

'I am here, Mrs Smith, respecting the sad occurrence of yesterday. Can you tell me anything relating to it?'

'I am afraid no more than you already know, Sir Edward,' said Mrs Smith, putting down the child in a chair; 'but I can't help thinking about it. Poor fellow, it makes me quite miserable! How it could have happened I can't make out.'

'It was quite an accident, of course,' said Sir Edward.

'I suppose it was.'

'You do not think he did it purposely?'

'Well, Sir Edward, I'm sure I don't know. Sometimes I think he did, but Smith says I have no business to think so ; but how should he know any better than I do ?'

'How, indeed?' said Sir Edward, 'for though he may have seen more of him than you have, he may not have observed as much.'

'I don't know, Sir Edward.'

She felt that they were getting upon tender ground, and in consideration for the feelings of her companion, she would not say that she thought he had grown desperate from having been crossed in love, though the words were ready on her tongue for utterance.

'Shall I take the child ?' asked Miss Montag.

'Yes, do ; please take him upstairs, and bathe his eyes.'

This was more than she desired, and for once in her life she unwillingly complied with the good lady's request. The idea that, as soon as she was gone, Mrs Smith would speak more freely about Philip, than she would have done in her presence, made her tremble so much that her legs seemed almost unequal to the task of carrying her upstairs. She had, however, scarcely reached the topmost step when she heard the voice of Smith near the house, and at once grew stronger. She knew Mrs Smith would not talk over freely of her domestic affairs in his presence.

'I am very sorry, Sir Edward,' said Smith, 'that you have been kept waiting. I did not expect you down before eleven o'clock.'

'I have been well entertained,' was the reply; 'but I came early that you might show me the place of the accident before it could be much changed.'

When they reached the spot, Sir Edward looked searchingly around. Everything in the neighbourhood of it served only to confirm his fears. Besides the dense wood by their side, the bushes and trunks of the lofty elms would afford shelter for any one bent on mischief.

'I suppose your assistants are all about their work this morning?' he said thoughtfully.

'All but the one on the sick-list,' replied Smith.

As Sir Edward was returning to the Hall, he was met by Oliver and Jesse with the intelligence that Lea had reached home from the hospital, but quite unable to give a correct account of what had during the night been passing near him.

'We must leave him to himself for a while, I am afraid. His only motive for coming back that we can learn,' said Jesse, 'has been to ask your permission for his immediate return to the hospital, to watch over his son.'

'Poor fellow!' said Sir Edward, 'I ought to have sent to him the first thing this morning, to say he might remain there as long as the doctors would permit him.'

'I was going to suggest it to you last night, papa,' said Oliver, 'and to offer to go myself; but I concluded, if it were right, you would think of it yourself.'

Sir Edward looked at his weak son for a moment, and then said,—

'Thank you; I wish you had, Oliver.'

The sound of the name at the end of the sentence left the lips of the father in so gentle and loving a manner, that the young man turned away to hide the tears that came unbidden to his eyes.

Sir Edward, on entering the library, was immediately followed by Lea.

'I am sorry to see you so much distressed,' said Sir Edward.

'May I go back to him?' was the answer.

'Oh yes, of course, if you desire to go; but you are, I trust, satisfied that your son is receiving proper attention at the hospital?'

'Yes, Sir Edward; but he is very bad.'

'Has he recognised you?'

'No; he has not yet once opened his eyes.'

'Then he is not conscious?'

'The doctors say he is not.'

'And they think he is in a dangerous state?'

'Yes; and he may not live till I get back. Please let me go.'

'I am afraid,' said Sir Edward, 'you are letting your excited feelings rob you of your judgment. If I thought you could be of the slightest service there, I would not keep you here a moment longer, but—'

'Oh, Sir Edward,' cried Lea, interrupting him, 'you know how I have loved my boy. Can I suffer him to die without being by his side to commend his soul to God, and say I forgive him for any wrong he has done me?'

'Do the doctors think there is any chance of his regaining consciousness?' asked Sir Edward.

'They said it was possible.'

'Go, then, by all means. How did you come back?'

'In a trap from the town.'

'The horse will be unequal to the return journey without rest. The coachman shall drive you over; and perhaps you and Jesse would like to go with him,' he said, turning to Oliver.

' I shall be pleased to go,' said Oliver.

'And I too,' added Jesse.

' Then away with you all to the stable,' said Sir Edward, 'that no time may be lost. If anything particular happens while you are there, you can let me on the instant have notice of it. You must not be late home.'

A minute more and Sir Edward was alone, while his late suppliant, with Oliver and Jesse, were running to the stable to get the coachman, with the carriage, on the road as quickly as possible.

CHAPTER II.

POOR Lea, who had always been less remarkable for the strength of his mind than the tenderness of his heart, had during the last few hours suffered more than any one unacquainted with such a temperament as his could easily imagine. For years his son's behaviour had been to him a source of endless trouble and bitterness of spirit.

The slightest extra show of affection on his part to the self-willed, misguided youth, had only appeared to produce in return a feeling of undisguised disgust—the more humiliating from the sneer at the occupation of his father with which it was accompanied. Still his strong affection remained undiminished, or rather, it may be said, to have been ever on the increase, growing in strength by feeding on the very obstacles that seemed to threaten its destruction.

It is generally taken as granted that men in Lea's station of life are not troubled with much refinement of feeling ; but whether the common consent to such a proposition is correct or not, we will not stop to inquire. It would doubtless admit of argument, and therefore it must suffice for our present purpose when we state the fact as it appeared in Lea, that, from a child, he had given repeated evidence that, however lowly his position in the world might be, he possessed a tender and generous heart.

For the development of his natural inclination, he was at one period of his life doubtless favoured by circumstances which, by his own skill, he had no hand in fashioning.

On the death of the late Sir Henry Harewood, he eagerly embraced the opportunity that was then presented to him of entering into the service of the new baronet, and of going with him, as we have seen, on his twelve months' tour on the Continent. From his strict attention to his duties, he very shortly gained the favourable notice of his master, and was treated by him with what might be not unaptly called friendly confidence.

In their journeying in strange countries and amongst strangers, many incidents occurred that could not fail to make them feel their mutual dependence on each other, and awaken sympathies which might otherwise have remained dormant. At length the kindly feeling thus engendered between them became so strongly marked, that the mere serving man was the acknowledged humble friend of the master, though, in the presence of visitors, their relationship, as the world would have it, was never lost sight of.

Shortly after his return with Sir Edward from his tour, he married, and had the misfortune to lose his wife immediately after she had given birth to a son. His grief for his great loss was slightly mitigated when he took his child in his arms and thanked God that he was spared to him, happily ignorant of the unseen future which had now become a fearful present.

On the instant he resolved that, in as far as he could, his son should not miss the nursing and tender care of a mother. A nurse was found in whom he had full confidence, and who, as months and years passed away, proved herself worthy of the trust reposed in her. On her part, it was not a mere mercenary engagement. She had buried her own child, and she then took the little stranger to her bosom to fill the void place that had been left there by her loss. Yet, in after years, by the in- gratitude of the youth, she felt she was but ill repaid for the watchful care she had so unselfishly bestowed upon him.

Ere the boy could be well trusted to run about the house alone, his intelligent counten- ance obtained the favourable notice of all that looked upon him ; and many were the compli- ments bestowed upon his beauty which, happily, he could not then understand, or they might not have passed him harmlessly by. Too soon, however, he became conscious that, in the estimation of those around him, he was no common child, which, of course, did not tend to his advancement in unselfishness.

But, as a sad portend to his future career, it might have been observed that, as he in- creased in years, the growth and strength of his intellect was unfortunately unaccompanied by moral qualities of corresponding force, and hence the commendations that were bestowed upon him for his encouragement to persevere in his studies, that he might be prepared for a useful race in life, fell far wide of their aim.

He became proud and conceited, with a disposition to think that the world was made for his special benefit, so that he could not help looking down with contempt upon those who, from father to son, were content to go on in the old plodding way for the mere necessaries of life. At school he placed himself, almost without an effort, at the head of his class, and thereby obtained the encouraging notice of his masters, and, through them, a greater hold upon the mind of his patron, Sir Edward Harewood, who was willing, under any circumstances, to look with favourable interest upon the boy from the respect he bore to his father. But the student did not trouble himself about that. He took every smile and commendation that was unsparingly bestowed upon him, as his natural right, arising from his own personal merit.

In one particular he was doubtless worthy of pity. His grandfather, the old steward, whose moral perceptions were none of the clearest, as his temper was not of the best, appeared with increasing years to be growing wayward, if not childish, in his proceedings. Through his penurious habits with all that related to his own expenditure, he had for many years been accumulating money until its care had become a burden to him.

There was no disguising the fact he was growing old. He could not keep the knowledge of it from any one. No, not even from himself. He could not for many more years hope or expect to retain the influence he had so long held in the Hall. Who was to take his place, and who was to get possession of his money? Who, but his son. He had no desire that any one other than his son should succeed him in his office, or take the purse that he had been so careful to fill. But he clung to life with the power he held so guardedly in his hands, and he could not look with complacency on the man, even though he was his own son, who was ready to step into his place at a moment's notice.

Allowing such thoughts to assert their supremacy, he became very jealous of his son's influence with their common master, and which he took no means to disguise from him. This state of things, much to the son's discomfort, very shortly after Sir Edward's return from his tour, unmistakably declared itself. As years passed on, the old man appeared to take increased pleasure in annoying his son, and, unfortunately for all parties, he was not slow to discover that his most vulnerable point for attack was through the boy Philip.

The father having observed the growing self-sufficiency of his boy, deemed it prudent to be less free with his commendations than he had hitherto been, and to refuse to supply him with pocket money, of which he would only make an ostentatious display, or part with it for some selfish indulgence.

Seeing this, the old steward kept the boy, when not at school, almost constantly by his side, and contrary to his habit and nature, grew very free with his money, and therefore made himself appear in the mind of the boy as very good-natured and liberal, the very opposite of the careful and cautious father. He never met him out of doors without having a piece of silver to put in his hand, even before he could ask for it, and when in his room he allowed him to do almost as he chose.

When his son strove to control his apparent generosity, he would growl out, ' I suppose you forget that you were a boy yourself once. But if you do, I don't. You were trouble enough to me, I know, though you do look upon yourself now as if you never committed a fault as a child, boy, or man in your life.'

For some time the son, hoping to bring about a more Christianly and better state of things, tried to argue with his father, and prove to him how injurious it must be to a boy like Philip, to let him feel that it was scarcely necessary for him to express a wish to have his wildest fancies gratified.

'You want to make him as tame as yourself, I suppose?' the old man would say; 'but it won't do. The boy has too much spirit to come down to your level.'

Disheartened and distressed, poor Lea at length gave up the struggle. He saw that anything he could say upon the subject, instead of winning his father over to a more reasonable mode of proceeding, only tended to confirm him in his purpose, and make the breach wider between them; and therefore while he continued ever watchful to promote the true welfare of his boy, he avoided speaking to his father on the subject in the earnest manner he had hitherto done.

It is only charitable to suppose that it was simply old age working upon the weakened brain of the steward, that made him feel and act so perversely. For although he was ever ready to treat his son's arguments as beneath contempt, or only to answer them by an ill-natured sneer, he was sorely provoked when they were discontinued, and he was left to pursue his own course with the boy unmolested, with anything more expressive than a pitying look.

When he had convinced himself that his power of annoying his son through his attention to Philip was gone, he entirely changed his behaviour. The boy was no longer welcomed to his room, and he would occasionally pass him in the village without a single word, or even a look of recognition.

Philip felt the change of treatment, although he could in no wise understand the cause that had led to it, and the effect it had upon his mind was most injurious. He looked upon himself as not only neglected but ill-used, and that it signified nothing what he might say or do, as he found he was in the end treated just the same, whether he tried to be agreeable or not; in short, that no one cared a straw for him, unless it was for the pleasure of pesting him with advice. Then he resolved that he must fight his own battle, and trust entirely to his own wits to help him on in the world.

He did not know that his prompters were pride and self-will. That in yielding himself up to their guidance he was laying the foundation of his building upon the shifting sands of deception, instead of upon the firm rocks of honesty and truth.

When, in the after part of his school days,

his father would say to him, 'God bless you,
my boy. I am sure you will do well, for
God is very good to us,'—he would answer,
'Oh yes; I mean to take care of myself.'
While, at the same time, he would think,
'I don't see what the good God has done
for me. You suppose, I daresay, that he has
been very obliging, and given me a good
father. But how do I look upon the gift?
Why, that I would rather never have had a
father than the one who seems proud to
show me at every turn that he is an ignorant
lout of a domestic servant. Yes, truly, I
have a great deal, no doubt, to thank God
for, though I cannot see exactly what it is
myself.'

Amongst his fellows at the superior school
to which he was sent to complete his education, he was constantly reminded of the out-
of-the-world position of his birth. While
one was talking of his father's hunters,
another of his mother's new carriage, and
another of the great deeds his uncle had
performed in the Indian mutiny, he could
not open his mouth respecting any one with
whom his parentage connected him without
prefacing his observation with a lie, or covering himself with confusion. His god was the

world, and although he was too proud to be
governed by any one in it, he was, perhaps
unknown to himself, immediately under its
influence.

When, through the indulgence of his ill-
trained and perverse will, he found himself
in difficulties in London, and circumstances
compelled him to call his friends to his assistance, a change for the better was apparent
in his behaviour. It lasted, however, but
for a short time. His heart had not been
touched; it was still the abode of selfishness,
and to all intents and purposes he held himself untrammelled by any conscious scruples
of morality or religion.

Sir Edward's kindness to the youth in
helping him out of his trouble went for
nothing, as he was reminded that it was
done, not for his sake alone, but rather out
of regard for his father. Yet for awhile,
on his appointment to his new office under
Smith, the novelty of wandering about the
grounds with a gun in his hand kept his dis-
contented spirit somewhat in check.

When alone he would fancy himself the
gentleman that he must inevitably, in the
course of years, become; look around at the
landscape, and consider what alterations it

would be necessary for him to make to improve its beauty, supposing his estate to be similar to the one he was now employed upon. But when his fellow keepers were with him the illusion passed away, and the stern reality of the present was pressed heavily on his mind. Their every word and look reminded him of who he was, and how far he was yet from the goal of his ambition.

His love for Miss Montag came upon him as something new, and which his mathematical knowledge did not help him to understand. The idea had never before entered his head that he could care for any one with a love equal to that he had for himself, or that he could be influenced by any other feeling than that of a due regard for his own personal interest. He had never dreamed that any young lady to whom he might be disposed to speak would not be too happy to welcome his addresses, and such being the case he was disposed to enjoy his freedom with them in common, as a young gentleman might happily do.

When he found himself being drawn within the influence of Miss Montag's gentleness, and she showed no disposition to encourage his advances, he was surprised and annoyed, and strove earnestly with himself to subdue his rising passion.   But it was not to be.   He could not refrain from looking at her when she was present, or have the picture of her features presented to his mind's eye when she was absent.   Then he became doubtful if she did not use every means in her power to avoid being left alone with him.   What could it mean ? Jealousy, as we have seen, came to his aid with an explanation, and determined him at length to put in force the scheme which he so utterly failed in carrying out to a successful issue.

The religious tone of his father's mind had caused him to look for true happiness in the right direction, and in the interest of his son all his energy had been spent to train him up for a life of usefulness.   He cared little about the kind of employment he should choose for himself when he was old enough to go out into the world, and take a part in its doings; so that it was healthful to him, and likely to prove beneficial to others, he would not attempt to influence him in the choice he should be able to make for himself.

On taking him to his first school, after he had passed the infant stage, the only request he made to the master was, that while he should be pleased to know that his boy was not overworked, he trusted that he would on no account be allowed to fall into habits of idleness. And again, when Sir Edward proposed to send him to a superior school, to the great delight of the youth, he offered no opposition to the plan, though, from his knowledge of the state of his son's mind, he had very serious doubts of its propriety. He knew more of the temper and disposition of his boy than Sir Edward dreamed of, but that he might not injure his future prospects, he was silent.

Very early he had observed what appeared to him the innate tendency of the boy's mind to selfishness, but he trusted the careful training he was receiving, combined with the influence of a good Christian education, would hold it in check, till as a man he could exercise his reason to control it, if not absolutely to cast it out of his heart altogether. Many times, from his boy's childhood, he had resorted to correction, both by word and act, with more or less severity, to convince him that an unbridled temper, governed by selfishness, could not fail to lead even one of the least of God's creatures into much unhappiness and trouble.

The poor father's doubts about the propriety of his son's removal to a higher school soon became apparent in the effect it produced to show that they had been only too well grounded. The demon pride accompanied him to his new home, and these, taking him by the hand, led him still further from the path of peaceful contentment. Then, during the school vacation, when he returned to Woodfield, it became a common remark of the villagers that he appeared ashamed of his old friends. However much of fancy there might be amongst them and the servants at the Hall, there was none on the part of the poor distressed father. The knowledge of his son's increasing pride had come to him as a sad reality. He had been spoken to by his son in a manner calculated to wound him more deeply than as if a dagger had been plunged into his heart. The one would but kill the body, but the other tortured the soul.

And this from the child whose welfare he had studied from his cradle, whose every want had been anticipated, and every ill that could threaten provided against. One whom he had loved as his own soul, and on whose lips he had seen reflected back, as if from another world, the smile of his angel mother. It was hard, very hard to bear, and yet he had silently borne it until his heart was nearly broken.

We will not follow the poor father through the ward of the hospital to the bedside of his son. Once there, seeing he could do nothing to alleviate his sufferings, he sat hopelessly down, and remained' for many hours almost motionless, eagerly watching for the first sign of returning consciousness, which he was never more to see. It might require time to finish the work, but the death-blow had been struck, and every ambitious thought for ever silenced in that self-seeking brain.

Oliver and Jesse having performed their task by leaving Lea at the appointed place, and given their horses a good long rest, walked back to the hospital, and there learning that the wounded youth still lay in the utmost danger, returned home to Woodfield with the cheerless intelligence.

Little conversation passed between the brothers by the way. Oliver was never one to originate a conversation of any length, and now he appeared to have little or nothing to say, while Jesse remained almost silent. The accident seemed to have produced a greater effect upon his mind than might have been expected, considering the general buoyancy of his spirits, and the hopefulness of his nature.

When they were near home they met one of the under keepers going along the road with his

gun thrown carelessly over his shoulder. As
they passed him Oliver shuddered, and said,—

‘ I am afraid I shall never take a loaded
gun in my hand again without trembling,
lest I should shoot myself, or some one
else.’

‘ You need have no fear,’ said Jesse, ‘ if you
are careful. You must never have your gun
on full cock until the instant you are about to
fire. It is a very simple precaution, and for
want of observing it many sad accidents are of
daily occurrence.’

‘ But one cannot always be so thoughtfully
careful,’ replied Oliver. ‘ Very often when I
am expecting I shall soon have to fire, I hardly
know what I am doing.’

‘ You must not speak like that at home,’ said
Jesse.

‘ No,’ replied Oliver, with a sigh, ‘ I know it
would make my father angry.’

‘ You must endeavour to get the mastery of
your fear,’ said Jesse.

‘ I am always trying to do so,’ rejoined
Oliver.

‘ Yes,’ said Jesse, ‘ and I think you were
going on very well till yesterday ; but now, if I
am to trust to what you say, you are losing
ground again.’

' And I am afraid,' sighed Oliver, ' this terrible accident has made you a little nervous.'

' Well, perhaps it has,' said Jesse, in a tone very different from that which he usually employed.

CHAPTER III.

PON receiving a report the next morning from the hospital that the death of the wounded youth was only a question of time,—that nothing short of a miracle could keep him alive but a few days longer at the most—Sir Edward mounted his horse and rode over to see the surgeon, and to learn from him if there was any chance of the return of consciousness before the end declared itself in death.

He felt that it was of the utmost importance that he should have the deposition of Philip of the real cause and manner of the accident. A few words, however, from the surgeon assured him that there was little or no chance of his ever speaking again, but that if the unexpected should occur, he should be without fail immediately informed of the fact.

The battle between life and death lasted for

a week. Then came the end, but so quietly that the father, who still sat by the side of the bed, knew not the moment when his son ceased to breathe. While life lasted he felt a glimmering of hope fluttering about his heart, and kept to his post, despite the mental and physical weakness from which he was suffering; but when he saw that all was over, his strength of body and mind alike forsook him, and he became for a while almost as inanimate as his son.

When he returned to himself he cried out, like David of old,—' Oh, my son, my son!' and then quietly left the hospital, unfit as he was, to resume his duties at the Hall.

The next day but one was appointed for the inquest. Sir Edward had continued his searching inquiry into the cause of the accident, but had in his own mind arrived at no satisfactory conclusion respecting it. There was still something strange about it which he could not understand, and that arose chiefly from the fact that the father of the deceased youth was reported as the first to be on the spot after the fatal shot had been fired.

How came he to be there, and what further information he could give on the subject, Sir Edward was most desirous of learning; but while the struggle was going on at the hospital he forbore to question the father, but he could do so now no longer. He felt that he should be made acquainted with every particular before the meeting of the jury, that he might not be surprised by anything that should come out before them with which he was not able, if requested, to give a satisfactory explanation.

All, however, he could learn from Lea was that he was out for a walk alone, and then that when standing on a hill he had seen his son near the wood, and was going down to speak to him, when he heard the report of a gun, and ran to the spot where he saw the smoke coming through the bushes, and where he was found by his young masters and Smith.

Sir Edward, seeing that the poor fellow was greatly excited, and that the picture called up before him was causing him a fearful amount of mental agony, desisted from further questioning. He was also partly induced to take the course he did from his knowledge that Lea would shortly be questioned by the coroner, when, if there was any further information to be obtained from him, it must come to light.

Although the whole occurrence may, in the eyes of a stranger, appear altogether but a very trifling affair, at a time when it is no uncommon thing to hear of a ship going down to the bottom of the sea with hundreds of passengers ; or trains crashing together on the railway, at the expense of many lives and much suffering ; or fires sweeping away almost entire cities ; or mountains toppling over from their giddy heights on the dwellers in the valleys below ; or earthquakes and floods devastating whole regions of the earth ;—still, in the present case, there was enough to call together at the inquest a crowd of the curious, who appear to be ever on the watch to hasten to the spot where a sad event has taken place or is to be investigated.

The jury being assembled, and all due formalities attended to, the coroner in a brief address placed the case before the court.

As the reader is already acquainted with most of the particulars to be brought before the jury, it will not be necessary to repeat the evidence of more than a few of the witnesses. The first of these was the surgeon, who readily confirmed what the coroner had said respecting the cause of death ; but when he was asked if the wound was of such a nature that it must have arisen from the accidental explosion of the wounded man's own gun, he hesitated to give a decided answer.

That it was the result of such an accident he thought was most probable, but, for anything he could say to the contrary, the gun might have been discharged by the unfortunate man himself, or by some one else at a short distance from him.

Oliver was the next witness called, who answered briefly to the questions put to him, as did also Jesse and Jasper.

Smith was questioned closely as to whether he or any of his party was separated from the others during the time they were out, to which he could only reply that they were generally together, though they might at times be hidden from each other by the trees and bushes.

'Can you say whether or no it was during your separation the shot was fired?'

'I cannot,' replied Smith, 'for as far as I have been able to make out no one heard it. There was a strong breeze blowing through the wood at the time, and making a great noise with the dry leaves.'

When the poor father rose in answer to his name, his appearance excited universal sympathy. He was very pale, and held on to the back of the chair for support. His eyes were red, and his lips quivered with emotion, but it was evident to all present that he was making a strong effort to appear calm.

'You were with your son when the accident occurred, were you not?' said the coroner very gently.

'Not with him, but I had seen him a short time before.'

'Will you tell us where?'

'Near the spot where I afterwards found him. I had occasion to walk in that direction. When on a hill, I saw my son down in the valley, and as I wished to speak to him, I hastened towards him.'

'And you heard nothing?' said the coroner.

'Yes, I heard the shooting party,' he replied in a tone of despair.

'When you first saw your son, was he quite alone?'

'Yes, quite.'

'And you saw no one else near at the time?'

To that question the poor fellow appeared unable to reply. He became faint, and would have fallen to the floor had not a gentleman who stood near supported him. Seeing that all eyes were fixed upon him, he earnestly strove to recover his self-possession, and after having sipped a little water from a glass that was presented to him, he said,—

'Before I saw my son, I saw two other persons in the valley at a little distance.'

'Were they together?' asked the coroner.

'No; when I first saw them they were some distance from each other.'

'Did they meet?'

'Yes, and then disappeared together.'

'Do you know who they were.'

'I could not swear to them.'

'But you think you know them.'

'Yes.'

'Will you tell me their names.'

'I think one was Mr Jesse Harewood, and the other Dixon, one of the under keepers.'

'And did you see them again?'

'Yes, almost immediately.'

'What took place then?'

'I saw a hare start from a bush, at which Mr Jesse fired, but did not hit it. Then I heard a very loud report, and I think Dixon shot the hare, for I saw him pick up something from the ground, and with Mr Jesse again disappear behind the trees.'

As he finished speaking, his emotion almost stopped his utterance. A horrible dread had taken possession of his heart that he would be forced to repeat all that he had seen his son attempt to do. To declare what he felt was the truth would be to proclaim his son to be a murderer, at least in intention, and not to speak the truth would be to render himself despicable in his own eyes as long as he lived.

His brain reeled under the weight that pressed upon it, while a dimness came over his eyes which rendered everything indistinct before him. It soon became evident that he was not in a fit state, even if physical weakness did not prevent him, for answering at the present time any further questions.

He was led out from the room in a very helpless state, and for many days afterwards was a patient suffering from brain fever, under the same roof where he had so lately watched by his dying son.

The inquest, however, was not immediately adjourned. Smith was recalled and questioned as to the length of time Mr Jesse and Dixon were out of his sight, but he was not able to give a satisfactory answer. He could only reply generally that it could not at any one time be more than a few minutes. He had heard the two shots fired spoken of by the last witness, and he understood that Dixon had shot a hare, which Jesse also, on being recalled, confirmed.

Smith was asked if he had reason to believe that his men were generally on good terms with each other; but his answers appearing unsatisfactory, one of the under keepers was called and closely questioned upon the subject, and after fencing about a good deal, admitted that they did not agree very well together, and further, that he had heard threats of personal violence used on both sides between Philip and Dixon, and once he had heard one of them say the other ought to be shot.

' And which one said that?' asked the coroner.

' Dixon,' said the man ; ' but I believe it was only as a jest.'

Then Jesse was again recalled to know if, after the two shots spoken of, he and Dixon continued together until the wounded man was found.

Jesse could not speak with certainty to the fact, but he believed they did, as they almost immediately afterwards joined the others of their party.

It was a little unfortunate for Dixon that he was not to be found when his name was first called by the coroner, which occasioned him to be passed over, while grave doubts were

rising in the minds of several of the jurymen to
his prejudice as they listened to the evidence
brought out from the other witnesses, so that
when he appeared in the room he was looked
upon by them with a certain amount of suspicion as to whether the fatal shot had not
been fired from his gun.

The coroner was not free from the doubt, as
was apparent, when on addressing Dixon, he
said,—

'Before I take your evidence, I think it right
that I should warn you that as you were one
of the persons last seen near the wounded man,
and that you had not been living on very
friendly terms with him, you need not answer
any questions put to you unless you like, but
that whatever you do say will appear in my
notes, and may at some future time be brought
forward against you.'

'Were you in company with the deceased
before he fell?'

'No, I had not even seen him that morning.'

'You mean the morning he was shot?'

'Yes.'

'We have heard from one witness, who, unfortunately, was not able to finish his evidence,
that you were seen near him with your gun in
your hand.'

'My occupation required me to have my gun,' said Dixon, 'but whether or no Philip Lea had any business there with his, perhaps Mr Smith can tell you better than I can.'

'Was he not like yourself, one of the keepers?'

'He had been, but I was told that morning he had left his employment and gone to London.'

'This is something new,' said the coroner, 'but it does not affect the main question. Were you on friendly terms with Philip Lea?'

'No, not very, and I don't know any one that was,' replied Dixon in a careless tone. 'He thought too much of himself for us, and was always ready to quarrel with any one who came in his way.'

'Did you ever quarrel with him?'

'We may have had a few cross words together,' said Dixon in his former tone.

'But you did not fight?'

'No, we talked of knocking each other down, but we never did it.'

'That will do,' said the coroner. 'I will not trouble you with any more questions at present.'

Smith was again recalled, and said it was quite true that he had told Dixon of Philip Lea's departure for London.

' Then, at the time of his being shot, you did not know that he was upon the premises ? '

' No ; I thought he was in the train for London.'

' But how, then, do you account for his being where he was found with the gun by his side ? '

' I cannot account for it,' said Smith.

' Gentlemen of the jury,' said the coroner, ' owing to the breaking down of one of the witnesses, I am afraid we shall not be able to finish the present inquiry to-day. In the course of an hour I must be at another inquest at some distance from this place. I must ask you, therefore, to agree with me for an adjournment for a week. I will not now make any comment on what we have heard ; but I may just remark that there are some parts of the evidence to which we have been listening to a little perplexing. I, however, trust that the explanation which may yet be forthcoming from the father of the dead man, will prove to your satisfaction that the case we have to deal with is purely the result of an accident, caused by the incautious use of firearms.'

The business of the inquest being over for the day, endless were the comments made upon it by the crowd that had been drawn together in and around the place.

'I wouldn't be in Dixon's shoes for a trifle,' said one man to another, 'and the best thing he can do is to make himself scarce while he has a chance.'

'But if he knows no more about the affair than he says he does,' said the one addressed, 'he is not the fellow to make himself scarce. He knows too well the value of a good name to run away and leave a bad one behind him.'

'Well, bad or good,' said the first speaker, 'if it were my case, I should look to my shoes and see if they were fit for a long journey, and keep my hat pretty near the door when it was not on my head.'

Another said, 'What a way Dixon's old mother will be in when she hears he is half suspected of having shot Philip Lea.'

'Yes, poor old body,' said another, 'it would almost frighten her to death no doubt if she thought there was any chance of his being guilty, but I know she will not believe it. She looks upon him as little less than an angel.'

'Rather a rough one,' said another.

'Not in her eyes,' was the answer.

And so the talk went on until the little crowd gradually melted away.

Meantime Sir Edward Harewood, avoiding his old friends as much as possible;. and particularly the coroner, with whom in the present state of affairs he had no desire to enter into conversation, set out with his sons immediately for home, deeply sympathising with poor Lea, whom he had been obliged to leave at the hospital.

The doubt that he had not heard a true account of the so-called accident, was rather strengthened than otherwise by what had come out before the coroner. When they had left the town and were fairly out in the country road, he remarked,—

'I am a little surprised, Jesse, that you did not tell me that you and Dixon were so near Philip when he fell.'

'I think, papa,' said Jesse, 'you will agree with me that I had good cause for my silence when I tell you that I did not know it myself.'

'You heard Lea's evidence ?'

'Yes; but, until he spoke, I had no idea of the fact. He appears to have seen all that passed; and I look upon it as very unfortunate that he was not able to finish his evidence.'

'You are quite certain that neither you nor Dixon saw either the father or the son ?'

'I can safely answer for myself,' said Jesse, 'and I think I can for Dixon.'

'It is, as you say,' observed Sir Edward, 'most unfortunate that Lea was not able to continue his account of what he had seen.'

'I think the coroner was very hard upon Dixon,' said Jesse. 'He made me feel quite angry with him, for I do not believe that Dixon had anything more to do with the shooting of Philip than I had.'

'I hope I did not say anything to injure him,' said Oliver.

'I think you scarcely mentioned his name.'

'I should be sorry to say anything to injure him, as he has always been very good and obliging to me.'

'And always at his own cost,' said Jesse, in a more cheerful tone than he had yet spoken. He saw his father looked thoughtful and anxious, and as he believed it was on account of his old favourite, whom he had been obliged to leave behind, he thought it better to introduce some light subject for conversation with Oliver than to make any allusion to the painful subject.

'Yes,' said Oliver; 'he generally has the worst of it when he comes to help me out of a difficulty. It was but yesterday he got into a bog nearly up to his neck, when he was showing me there was nothing to fear in passing over it.'

'I suppose he was too heavy to get safely over?' said Jesse.

'It was very good of him to go first,' said Oliver.

'I hope,' said Jesse to his father, 'that, notwithstanding the coroner's speech, you will let Dixon continue at his work.'

'I shall not stop him,' replied Sir Edward.

'And can any one else?' asked Oliver.

'I cannot say,' was the reply; 'we must wait to see what turn events will take.'

'I hope it will be a quiet turn,' said Oliver; 'and help us very soon to forget this sad affair.'

'And so do I,' said Jesse. 'It is quite bad enough as an accident, without speaking of it as a murder.'

'We must be careful of the use of that word,' remarked Sir Edward.

'I should never have thought of it,' said Jesse, 'if it had not been put into my head by the coroner.'

'He only spoke as he did,' rejoined Sir Edward, 'to make the investigation the more searching. Depend upon it, he has no desire to prove it a murder.'

On reaching home they found Mr and Miss
Gordon, with Charlotte and Grace, waiting impatiently for the news they would bring them ;
for, sad as they knew it must prove, it would
not be the less interesting.   For a full hour
it thrust aside all other questions, and particularly that part of it which related to Lea's
appearance before the coroner, with his sudden
illness and removal to the hospital.

'And have you really left him behind you ? '
said Grace to Jesse.

'Yes, I am sorry to say we have; but it
could not be helped.'

'Could we not have nursed him here ? ' asked
Grace.

'I thought we were to have brought him
back,' said Oliver; 'but I suppose it is best
as it is.'

The old steward made it his business to
hover about the speakers on one pretence or
another to catch up here and there a stray
word or sentence, but he did not show the
slightest disposition to ask any questions.
When told of his son's illness, he merely replied,—'Oh dear, that is bad ; but I can see
to his work here.'

His manner was strange in the extreme.
He appeared desirous of obtaining all the

information he could by indirect means, rather than by a simple question.

The excitement of the last few days had put its mark upon him, though not of the kind that might have been expected. His general bearing was a little more nervous than it had been of late; but at the same time his mental and physical powers seemed to have had a strong tonic applied to them by the increase of vigour he displayed. Had Sir Edward been less engaged with his own thoughts he might have observed the change, and complimented him on his improvement, but as it was, it was passed by him unnoticed. The young people, however, did not fail to see and comment upon it.

'Why, Mr Lea,' said Grace, on one occasion, when meeting him, 'upon my word you are getting quite young again, I do believe?'

' The times have driven me to it, miss.'

' The times!' repeated Grace. 'What do you mean?'

'Why, you see, miss, the things that are happening appear to make all the young heads shake on their shoulders. I mean the servants, of course; and if I were not to look after them a little sharper than usual, everything would get out of order.'

'Then it is lucky we have some old heads left,' said Grace, laughing.

'Yes, that's just it, miss,' was the satisfactory reply.

'I can't understand why Dixon is suspected of shooting Philip?' said Jasper to his master. 'You know he had no more chance of doing it than either of us, or Mr Jesse.'

'And I can't understand it either,' said Oliver.

'Why, we were nearly always together,' said Jasper, 'and when we were not, Mr Jesse was away as much as any one, and who would suspect him?'

'No one, of course,' said Oliver.

'Then I want to know why Dixon should be suspected?' said Jasper.

'I cannot answer you,' rejoined Oliver, 'but I know I would not for all the world be one of the jury.'

'Oh, I would though,' cried Jasper, 'and I would say in a moment it was all an accident.'

'But if the others would not agree with you?'

'Then they might disagree.'

'But you would have to give in?' said Oliver.

'Would I, though?' said Jasper; 'they

might as well try to make a cat jump through a hoop backwards, as get me to say a thing was wrong when I knew it was right.'

At the expiration of a week the coroner again met the jury, and although Lea was still in the hospital, and unable to finish his account of what he had seen, the inquiry was proceeded with ; some fresh evidence was produced relative to the angry feeling that appeared to have existed amongst the under keepers, which increased the suspicion against Dixon, and caused the coroner in his summing up to speak of him in a very unfavourable manner.

Several of the jury, however, did not follow his lead. They thought the evidence was not strong enough to send him for trial, and for some time it was doubtful if there must not be another adjournment. The jury were divided into three parts. One was for bringing in a verdict of accidental death, the second of misadventure, and the last of wilful murder. At length they came to a compromise. It was known that the sessions were near at hand, and that the prisoner would not have long to wait for his trial, and it was therefore agreed that the verdict against Dixon should be for manslaughter.

CHAPTER IV.

THE verdict of the jury was severely commented on by the friends of Dixon, who clubbed their little means together, that he might have the benefit of counsel on the day of his trial. They knew that any other plan they might adopt to save him must prove futile. That an attempt to show that he had been unjustly committed must end in failure, and that the verdict having been once given, the only chance there was of successfully opposing it would be at the trial.

Oliver was greatly surprised at the result of the inquiry, and as for Jasper, he was furious and dared not speak of it, but to an old crony in her house, where he could give vent to his opinion without reserve. He had conversed with Oliver, who agreed with him, but who was too timid to listen to his bold assertions lest it should get to the ears of his father, and he should be again reprimanded for being on too familiar terms with his servant.

To avoid being brought into trouble in that way, Oliver would have kept constantly close to his brother, but he was painfully convinced that Jesse did not want his company. The next best thing he thought he could do was to keep in the presence of his sisters as much as possible. This led him to take many walks with Charlotte and Miss Gordon in their visits to the sick and poor of the parish.

He was not at all times quite at his ease with them. Their conversations were often a little above his comprehension. But there was no help for it, as Grace was at her lessons, and he must either go out with them or wander about alone, which he knew, from experience, he could not easily do, as Jasper would be sure, by some means or other, to find out his whereabouts, and come to him to know if he was wanted.

Sir Edward brooded in silence over the doubts that still clung to his mind. Like Jasper, he could not see why Dixon should be suspected more than others. Still, it was a great relief to him to know that not a shadow of suspicion had in the public mind fallen upon Jesse, and which made him willing to leave the event in the hands of the judge who would have to try the case.

When Jesse, who took an active part in getting in subscriptions for the defence of Dixon, appealed to him for assistance, he excused himself for not opening his purse by saying that as a magistrate, and one so nearly connected with the case, he thought it would not be right to take part in the popular movement, but he did not convey to the mind of the petitioner that he disapproved of what he was doing.

Jesse's exertions in favour of the prisoner had been greatly stimulated by his visits to the keeper's house. Smith could not believe in Dixon's guilt, but he was cautious in his words respecting his opinion, and felt also constantly obliged to warn his wife of the consequence of her speaking so freely, as she was disposed to do, upon the question before it was finally decided in a court of justice. She believed Philip shot himself out of sheer despair about Miss Montag. That jealousy had driven him to madness, but she knew the man he was jealous of was not Dixon. Still, she could not say who it was without doing an amount of mischief which she shrank from ; and so it happened that, when she spoke of it, she became confused, and then, not to draw attention to her thoughts, she would go off into warm denunciations against the jury, and by so doing make her husband very angry.

But it was neither Smith nor his wife who gave the life - spring to Jesse in his endeavours to serve Dixon. He had spoken to Miss Montag about him, and learnt from her how earnestly she desired his acquittal.

'It is very unfortunate for the poor fellow himself,' she said, 'that he should be charged with such a crime ; but for his poor mother, it appears little short of death. She was here yesterday, the picture of misery. She did not believe in her son's guilt, but she said she pictured him to herself, night and day, shut up away from the woods of which he was so fond, pining in silent despair. " Gladly would I," she said, with tears in her eyes, " go and be shut up where he is if they would let him out. I know he would not run away and leave me there." '

'Poor body,' said Jesse, 'I am afraid we can do nothing for her but preach patience, and I should be a poor hand at that were I to meet her.'

'She was not noisy in her grief,' said Miss Montag, 'but I think she was nearly broken-hearted. I do not know what she would do if her son's weekly money was not given to her.'

'I am glad Smith has the order to pay her that, and that he will continue to do so, at the least, till after the trial.'

This meeting of Jesse and Miss Montag out in the private road that ran through the park, was mere chance on her part, but whether it was entirely so on his may be very questionable. Of late he had appeared to take great pleasure in wandering about the grounds alone, with his gun as his only companion. He told Smith he did not want him, and if he met any of the under keepers in his rambles he dismissed them with a few words and strolled away.

Mrs Smith's eyes were getting wider open every day, but what could she do to stop the current of events. If she spoke to Smith she knew he would only laugh at her, and for her speaking to Sir Edward, that was quite out of the question. She trembled to think of the confusion it might occasion, not only at the Hall, but between her husband and herself. As for Miss Montag, whom she had learnt to love as a daughter or a sister, it would prove little short of ruin. The honest body became greatly exercised in her mind, and, after much thought, decided on a plan which, while the knowledge of it was confined to her own bosom, would enable her to separate them for some time.

In furtherance of her plan, she said to her husband,—

'Georgie does not appear to be getting up his strength at all nicely. I think I will ask the doctor if a little change of air would do the child good.'

'Doctors don't send their patients away when their friends can pay for them at home,' said Smith.

'You must not be so hard upon the doctor,' rejoined his wife; 'and, if you do not object, I will ask him what he thinks about a change for the dear little fellow.'

'But where could you go?' asked Smith.

'To your brother at Brighton.'

'To a confectioner's shop!' said Smith; 'just the very place to send a sick child for a change.'

'We would take care that he did not get too many sweets.'

'We,' said Smith. 'You speak as if I was going with you.'

'No; I know you could not go.'

'And I don't see,' said Smith, 'how you could go and leave all the other children behind.'

'The others will go to school; but I did not mean that I would go to Brighton myself. I thought we might send him with Lizzie. She has not been looking very well lately, and a little change might do her good.'

'But would she like to go?' asked Smith.

'I have no doubt she would, if she thought it would do the child good,' answered Mrs Smith confidently. 'When I have spoken to the doctor I will ask her.'

'Better ask her first.'

'Then,' said Mrs Smith, 'if the doctor said no she would be disappointed, all for nothing.'

'Well, as you like,' said Smith. 'I have quite enough to do out of doors, without troubling you or myself about what you do within.'

So the question remained until the doctor was consulted, when his opinion, proving favourable to Mrs Smith's wishes, her scheme was rapidly carried out, and Miss Montag found herself with her charge safely at

Brighton, greatly to her own satisfaction as well as the child's.

For some weeks she had been living in a state most difficult for a young person of her age and temperament to endure. Her connection with Philip Lea had been, as we know, of a very painful character. For awhile after his death she was almost beside herself from her fear that she would be called upon as a witness at the inquest. Happily for her her fears had been groundless.

Then there was the new sensation struggling in her breast which she could scarcely understand herself, and dared not speak of to another. That Jesse gladdened her eyes when he appeared before her, and that a chance touch of his hand sent a thrill through her nerves was beyond question. She could not blind herself to the fact, though she felt she would rather die than let any one else share her secret. Mrs Smith was very kind to her, and any secret short of this she would have freely trusted to her keeping.

Then she would ask herself if Jesse had given her reason to think of him as she did. He had always been gentle and kind in his speech with her, but was he not so with every one? She had seen him with his sisters and

Miss Gordon, and she could not see that he had been more kind to her than he always appeared to be to them.

And then even if he had paid her marked attention, what could she hope it would lead to? Was he not the favourite son of Sir Edward Harewood? and had not fortune marked him out as one whose natural place would be in the higher circles of society? And what was she? An unknown orphan, so poor that she did not even know her own name. Pleasing as the dream would sometimes be of being loved by such a man as Jesse, it would be nothing short of madness for her to think of it as a reality.

It was, therefore, with a strange feeling of relief from her perplexities that she heard of her journey to Brighton. So far was she from showing any disinclination to leave home, that she freely expressed the pleasure it would give her to take the little fellow to the sea-side and keep him there as long as they chose. She spoke in so hearty a manner, that the planner of the project began to think she had over-shot the mark and formed a love-making business, which only existed in her own imagination.

'We live in a world of gossip,' she said to

her husband. 'Why should we say the child is going to Brighton. We don't want any excursionists to call and see him there, and I daresay your brother don't either.'

'Unless they go for refreshment in the way of business,' suggested Smith.

'And to pay for it,' rejoined his wife. 'Yes, but they would do no such thing. They would call out of respect to you, and take a friendly cup of tea. My opinion is we had better not say where he is going, and then we shall not be tormented by people offering to take messages for us, or get any brought back to us.'

'As you please,' said Smith. 'I don't think it signifies much which way it is.'

'Then we will only say he is gone away for change of air, and leave the curious ones to find out where.' Of course she did not make the slightest allusion to Jesse, though he of all the people in the parish was the one most in her thoughts.

While Mrs Smith was so busy with her scheme to prevent mischief, affairs at the Hall were going on much in their usual course. Sir Edward continued to actively perform the duties pertaining to his position in society, as well as keep to the task he had taken upon himself on account of Oliver. For an hour, and sometimes two, on most evenings of the week he had him with him in his library, to converse upon subjects treated of in the various books he had desired him to read.

. The progress the young man was now making proved almost satisfactory to the father. He began to think that at last there was some chance of his being rewarded for the labour he had for so long bestowed upon him. There was one thing, however, which had again come before him, of which he could not approve, and that was the great familiarity with which he treated his servant Jasper. To remedy this, he said one evening to Oliver, ' Your little man, as I used to call your servant, is, I think, getting too old for what you require of him. A boy of the size he was when he came to you would answer your purpose very well, and then Jasper would be able to get a better situation.'

This happening at the time when Oliver, for his own comfort, was keeping as much as he could apart from Jasper, did not sound so harsh to him as it might otherwise have done. On the contrary, he was pleased with the idea. As he was being gradually drawn more towards his sister and Miss Gordon, he felt less need of

the society of Jasper, and answered his father
very readily, by saying,—

'I shall be very glad to see Jasper get a
better place.'

'Perhaps you will tell him so,' said Sir
Edward.

'I will do so, if you please.'

'Of course you will speak kindly to him,
and not let him feel that because you do not
require his services any longer, you are careless
of what becomes of him.'

'I should be sorry to do so,' replied Oliver,
'for he has been a good servant to me.'

'This is better than I expected,' thought
Sir Edward.

Meantime Jesse continued his rambling
habits as usual, but they soon became unin-
teresting to him. The fair form that had
lighted up the landscape was no more to be
seen, and he felt that in the midst of his friends
he was alone. He called at the keeper's house,
but she was not to be seen there. He dared
not ask what had become of her, lest that
which was now so evident to himself should be
known by another.

On his second visit he missed the sick child;
then the truth dawned upon his mind that Miss
Montag was away from home with him. Of

the child he could speak without embarrass-
ment, although so much more was in the question than appeared on the surface.

'What have you done with Mr Georgie?' he
asked of the observant mother.

'Oh, poor little fellow, he has gone away
with Miss Montag for change of air, sir.'

'You could not trust him far away from you,
I should imagine?' observed Jesse.

'Oh yes, I can, sir; I know he will be quite
safe with her.'

'Of course he will,' replied Jesse.

He was about to add something which would
have led to a direct question for the address of
the missing pair, but he felt that he could not
do it without betraying more interest in the
subject than was desirable; he therefore re-
sisted the temptation, and resolved, if possible,
to conquer his desire to see them again.

His gun was forthwith left in its rest, and he
again returned to his reading with all his former
earnestness.   His father was not displeased to
observe the change.   He had encouraged him
after he had broken down from over-study to
keep out in the open air as much as possible,
but of late he had begun to fear that it was
leading him into idle habits, and that if he did
not soon return to his books, he would go to

Oxford very ill prepared to take the high place he had fondly imagined he would.

But after a few days had passed, everything was again changed. The pallid cheeks and the old wild look came back to the student's face; and it was evident to the least observant in the house that he was rapidly losing his health.

'This will never do, Jesse,' said his father to him one day; 'you are again working too earnestly with your books, and if you do not soon cool down a little, we shall have you under the doctor's hands once more.'

'I hope not,' replied Jesse wearily.

'Useful knowledge,' observed Sir Edward, 'is greatly to be desired, but it may be purchased at too costly a price, if it is gained at the expense of health. Put your books aside; I am not very busy to-day, and we will have an hour or two in the woods. Where is Oliver? We will not go without him.'

They went out, and sport was not wanting, but Jesse was far from displaying his wonted cheerfulness. Ever and anon, even when with his father, he would fall into fits of forgetfulness without any visible cause. Again and again he referred, in anxious, pitying tones, to the imprisonment of Dixon, and more than once drew Oliver, to his great disgust, to the scene of the late accident or murder, whichever it was to be called.

Sir Edward returned to the Hall, disappointed and perplexed. Jesse in his late illness, even when it was most serious, had looked hopefully forward to the time when he would be able to take his gun and go out into the open air, but now even that desire did not show itself. His step when moving about was listless in the extreme. Often when alone and in silence he had endeavoured to school himself for action by going direct to the keeper's house, and asking plainly, if not where they had sent their child to, when they expected him back.

'Yet what is the use of doing that?' he would murmur. 'They would know I was really inquiring for Miss Montag, whom I have so vainly striven to forget; and what would they say to me? Would they risk my father's displeasure by favouring my suit to her? But even if I could find her, would she receive me as a friend? and if she would not, how could I address her? Dare I speak to her from the prompting of my heart? Dare I tell her how much I love her? Should I so dare, what good would come of it? Would my father consent to receive her as a daughter?

I cannot hope he would. Well then, after
all, here is nothing better for me to do
than earnestly apply my mind to my book-
work, and leave no vacant place in my brain
or heart for fancy to continue her tormenting
work.'

Sir Edward not doubting but over-study was
causing the change in his manner and appearance, begged him to put his books away, and
take to his gun again, but without avail; then,
in despair of anything he could say or do himself, he rode over to his doctor to seek his
advice, when it was arranged between them
that he should call, as if by accident, at the
Hall, when he would be able to form an opinion
of the state of Jesse's health, and if he found
him suffering from any bodily disease, deal with
it on the instant.

'I am very anxious about my boy,' said Sir
Edward. 'This sad affair, which has had for
its result the death of one of my keepers and
the imprisonment of another, seems to be prey-
ing strangely on his mind.'

'Was he particularly attached to the dead
man?' inquired the doctor.

'No, I think not,' replied Sir Edward, 'nor
was I aware that he was so to the man Dixon,
who is now awaiting his trial, but by the in-

terest he now takes in him, it seems that he must have been.'

'He is of an age,' said the doctor, 'to have his sympathy aroused for one who, I understand, is generally considered to be suffering wrongfully. I suppose there is little chance of the man being convicted ?'

'It is a difficult subject upon which to give an opinion,' said Sir Edward; 'and I have sometimes felt sorry that my son has taken up the case so warmly, as it appears to have affected his health. I shall feel much more at my ease when you have seen him.'

'If nothing very unusual occurs,' said the doctor, 'I will be with you before twelve o'clock to-morrow, or I will go now, if you wish it.'

'Thank you,' said Sir Edward; 'but I think a casual call to-morrow, as you proposed, will be the best course to adopt.'

At the appointed time the doctor met Sir Edward and his two sons on the lawn.

'Why, young gentlemen,' he said playfully, after the greetings of the morning were over, 'you appear to have changed places since I last saw you—while Mr Oliver is looking better than I ever saw him before; you, on the contrary,' he said to Jesse, 'are looking as if you were having too much of your book-work again.'

'I am endeavouring to make up for lost time,' replied Jesse, with a forced smile.

'Yes,' remarked Sir Edward; 'he is so intent on his work that I had much difficulty to induce him to spend an hour with me out of doors this morning. I believe, if left to himself, he would remain in his room night and day.'

'He must not do so,' said the doctor. Then, addressing Jesse, he continued,—'I am only here as the friend to-day, but I warn you, if you attempt to work beyond your strength, you will shortly have me here again as the doctor.'

'I am ashamed of my weakness,' said Jesse.

'You have nothing to be ashamed of,' replied the doctor. 'You are not naturally weak; and if you will only be a little less eager in turning over the leaves of your book, you will do very well. You must remember you are not a mere machine, to be worked day and night without intermission.'

'I am afraid you give me credit for a greater desire for work than I possess; I often feel that I am very idle.'

'Well,' said the doctor, with a laugh, 'if you do not amend your ways, remember what I have said—expect the doctor back again in a very few days.'

After a little more talk to the same purpose, the visitor departed. Before he went, however, he said privately to Sir Edward,—

' If you cannot induce Jesse to resume his gun, the next best thing you can do is to send him from home for a time. He is evidently too much devoted to his books here. Let him go down to Brighton for a change. Besides the advantage of the bracing air, the bustle of the place will give him something new to think about. I have a friend there who will receive him, if you do not care to trust him in an hotel alone.'

' I thank you,' said Sir Edward ; ' but I think he would prefer going to an hotel. I can trust him anywhere, and he would doubtless feel under less restraint there than in a private house. You do not doubt his capability of taking care of himself?'

' Not in the slightest degree.' was the reply.

And so it was determined that Jesse should, without loss of time, set out for Brighton. When his father first spoke to him upon the subject, he showed but little concern about it. One place, he said, was the same to him as another ; and if he could only get rid of his present languid feeling, he would soon be all right again. But when he was told he must put aside his books and exert himself to throw off his languor, he instantly resolved that if he must be unhappy, he would not lay himself open to the pitying looks and soothing words of those around him. No; he would fight manfully against his despondency, and if he could not overcome it, he would, under a smiling face, bear with it in silence.

'I would let Oliver go with you,' said his father, 'only that, in your absence, I may want him with me at home ; but you can take his youth, Jasper, with you, if you like.'

'Thank you,' replied Jesse ; 'but I should prefer going alone.'

CHAPTER V.

T length the all - important day of Dixon's trial drew near, when the question which so deeply stirred the interest of the surrounding country was to be decided, either, as was supposed, in the liberation of the prisoner, or his being sent into penal servitude for life.

Circumstances had compelled Sir Edward to take a more prominent part in the matter than he had intended. To quiet Jesse, who continued very anxious about it, he had promised him before he set out for Brighton that Dixon should not be forgotten. He was still unfortunately under his old cloud of doubt, and therefore found himself in a very perplexing position when Jesse wrote from Brighton to say he must return for the trial, as he felt too greatly interested in the event to remain at a distance when it was taking place.

Sir Edward had a great objection to his son returning for such a purpose, and immediately answered his letter to beg him not to be anxious about the trial.

'You need not fear,' he wrote, 'that your absence will in any way prejudice the prisoner's defence. For myself, I can assure you I will not forget how earnest you are upon the subject, and that I will act for you as you would act were you here. You know a good advocate will conduct his defence; and though I may not be able to see the gentleman myself, I will employ a friend whom I know I can trust to carry out my instructions. Having made these arrangements chiefly on your account, I must therefore beg you not to think of returning home for the present.'

When the letter reached Jesse, it made him feel very angry. From the tone in which his father had written, he saw that he was expected to take his begging him not to return as a command not to do so. He was not absolutely angry with his father, but rather with the circumstances in which he found himself so disagreeably placed. The noise and constant change going on in the hotel and the streets had in some measure diverted his thoughts from the old story, but they quickly lost their influence over him, and he began to feel as much alone as he would have done in his father's woods.

Before answering his letter, he strolled out to the beach to muse on the nature of his reply, and then returned to his hotel to perform his task. The letter went by the evening post, but it was written in a far different spirit to what it would have been had not the recollection of an incident which happened to him while he was out been present to his mind.

A short time before the trial Lea, who had nearly recovered from his late illness, at his earnest request was permitted to return to the Hall. He was still very weak, but it was thought the change might prove beneficial to him, and help him to meet with less pain his ordeal before the court on the appointed day. His appearance proved very unsatisfactory to his kind-hearted master. He did but half respond to the hearty welcome he received, and the warm sympathy bestowed upon him on his return. Though he was gaining strength in his body, his spirits were very much depressed, and nothing that could be said or done was able to bring a smile to his face.

Thinking that time would do more than any

amount of talking on his part, Sir Edward contented himself with an expression of his deepest
sympathy, and then appeared not to notice the
sad looks and nervousness of his old favourite.
He knew nothing of the struggle that was
taking place in the poor fellow's mind — a
struggle the intensity of which few are called
upon to wage with the unseen enemy of our
race, though too many have to contend with his
suggestions of what the world will say or think
of them if they do not attempt to blind it by a
departure from the truth.

He was not called upon to resume his active
duty. Sir Edward would occasionally have
him in his room, and speak kindly to him of
what they would do at some future time; but
he was, as he desired to be, generally left to
himself to mourn over the wasted life of his
son. At times his father would pay him a
visit, and worry him with his complaints of the
servants, and the little time the rascals gave
him to attend to his accounts, and see he was
not robbed by men who borrowed his money,
and wished to forget when the interest was
due.

'What the world is coming to I can't tell,'
he would say; 'but were I to go about with
only one eye open, I should be imposed upon at

every turn.   And then the men you have had under you are not worth their salt.'

'I always found them attentive to my orders.'

'Attentive to your orders!—of course they were,' said the old steward ; 'and why ? Why, just because you took care not to order them to do anything they did not like.'

'I think you are mistaken.'

'No, I am not, I tell you. You did not take the right course with them ; and if I had given them up, as you wished, entirely to you, we should have had the house out of windows by this time.'

'I am sorry you worry yourself so much about them.'

'Worry myself! How can I help it when I have to deal with such fellows ? Why, they take up all my time nearly to follow them about, so that I have scarcely any time to attend to my own business, and my papers are getting all scattered abroad, like dry leaves on a windy day.'

'I am sorry,' said Lea, turning restlessly in his chair, 'that I am not able to get about to help you, but if you will send them to me, I will speak to them.'

'Oh yes ; no doubt it would be very pleasant to you to speak softly to them, and make me appear an old stupid tyrant!'

'I do not deserve this from you.'

'Whether you deserve it or not, you must know what I think about your management, and how well you were fitted to get into my shoes, and take the whole upon yourself.'

'You will think better of me,' said Lea, 'some day, I hope, if I am spared to be with you.'

'Spared to be with me!' cried the old steward. 'I suppose you mean me to understand if I am spared to be with you? You want to remind me that I am an old man, and must soon give up all to you, but you may find yourself mistaken.'

'No,' replied the son faintly; 'I was speaking of myself.'

'And what reason have you to speak so? Just because you have been a little unwell about the loss of that graceless son of yours, that I always told you you did not know how to manage.'

'I must get out into the air,' said the sick man.

'You are a poor, faint-hearted creature,' said the old steward.

The night before the day fixed for the trial

the misery of Lea had become almost unbearable. The next day he must appear in court, and he had been assured by officious friends how much would depend on the evidence he had to give.

'Would to God,' he cried in his agony, 'I had never gone in search of that unhappy boy, and never seen what I did! And does it now really depend on what I shall say, whether the poor fellow Dixon is set at liberty or sent into perpetual banishment? What I have already said, I am told, will of itself go well nigh to insure his conviction. Must it be so? or shall I cover myself and my son's memory with a cloud by telling all I know of what really did take place on that fatal day? God help me! I am in a strait, and know not how to escape from it. If it were only a matter on which I could speak to a friend, and seek for advice; but it is not so; I cannot open my mouth without, I fear, proclaiming my poor boy a would-be murderer. I ask myself why he was found in the wood with a gun, when he had made every preparation for his journey?— why he had uttered threats of some mischief he intended to do? When he presented his gun at Dixon he did not fire. Was it because he was not the right person? Dreadful thought

—it must be so! Mr Jesse was the intended victim!'

Nearly on the verge of madness from his tormenting thoughts, he resolved, be the cost what it might to him or the memory of his son, he would open his heart to Sir Edward. He need only tell him what he had seen, without touching on his surmises, and so much of that only as would account for the accident.

Sir Edward listened to him very seriously. He was at first under the impression that he had lost his senses. If he had really seen the gun discharged in the hands of his son, why all this mystery respecting it? but when he remembered that he had been struck down by illness, and that Dixon had been committed for trial before he had sufficiently recovered to complete his evidence, he began to take a more rational view of the subject.

'I am sorry,' he said, 'you did not tell me this before; it would have relieved your mind, and I might have taken measures serviceable to Dixon, and made the coming trial less painful to you.'

'I have been very weak, and have not known what to do.'

'Then it was not mere chance that took you to the fatal spot?'

'No.; I went purposely in search of my son. I was told he was going away, and I wanted to persuade him not to go.'

'There is still the mystery of his being there with his gun after what he had said to Smith,' thought Sir Edward, but he made no allusion to it. He saw that Lea was not in a fit state then to be further questioned, and anything relating to that might be explained at some future time.

On the morrow the assize town was all in commotion. There were several cases down for trial, but in the minds of people generally that of Dixon's was the most serious.

Before the court was opened, Sir Edward, contrary to what he had proposed doing, sought an interview with the prisoner's attorney, and pointed out to him the additional evidence he had obtained in favour of the prisoner.

'If Lea is prepared to state on oath what you tell me,' said the attorney, 'the case may be considered over as soon as it comes before the grand jury. A true bill cannot be found against Dixon, and there the case will end. It will deprive my friend, Sergeant Bedford, of the opportunity of making a brilliant speech in favour of the prisoner, but he is too good a man to be annoyed on that account.'

The attorney judged correctly of the result. When the case came on in its turn before the grand jury, Lea, who had not completed his evidence at the inquest, was the first to be called.

The poor man entered the room pale and trembling. He had endeavoured to nerve himself for what he believed his duty with but little success. The horrible fear that his inmost thoughts respecting his son would be drawn from him he could not banish ; but, happen what might, he was fully resolved that he would not depart from the truth.

On his stating that he saw his son fall as the gun went off in his hand, the chairman asked him rather sternly why this evidence was not tendered before.

'I was too ill to give it.'

'But the inquest was adjourned.'

'Yes,' replied Lea ; 'but I was in the hospital and unconscious of what was taking place.'

'You say you saw the accident, and no one else was present ? '

'I saw the prisoner pass by a short time before, but he was not near when my son fell.'

'You were in company with your son ? '

'No ; I was near the place looking for him.'

'Gentlemen,' said the chairman, 'I think it

would only be waste of time to question the witness further. He says the death of his son arose from a pure accident, and that the man Dixon had nothing to do with it. I think if we have some of the other witnesses before us, and their evidence does not conflict with what we have just heard, the case will end with us, as it would be monstrous under the altered circumstances to find a true bill against Dixon.'

As Lea listened to what was said, a dimness came over his eyes, and he staggered to and fro like a drunken man, and then fell heavily to the floor. It was no fainting fit this time. The battle was over, and one more was added to the fathers who have died broken-hearted through the misconduct of a son.

But the business of the sessions must go on. The body of the dead man was carried out, and some more witnesses introduced; but the case was virtually at an end. 'No bill' was endorsed on the charge-sheet and sent up to the judge.

Very shortly afterwards Dixon was at liberty, greatly to the delight of his mother, and not a little to the disappointment of a group of ladies, who at great trouble had secured seats in the court to hear the trial, which would not now take place.

Sir Edward was greatly shocked on hearing of the sudden death of his faithful servant, and was disposed to blame himself very much for not having seen the dangerous state he must have been in since his return from the hospital. But if he had been deceived, the medical men had also, and that was some consolation to his wounded spirit.

Having secured a room where the body might remain till after the inquest, he returned home, with a heavy heart, to bear the sad news to the old steward—the father of him who would never more provoke him by trying to get into his shoes before he had done with them.

The old man received the news with an incredulous ear. He could not, or rather he would not, understand for some time that his son was dead. When he did realise the fact, and had been left by his master, he sat down in his easy-chair to think over the news he had been listening to, startling and unexpected as it was. That his son should have died in such a way amazed him much. He had never even dreamed of anything of the kind. Strange as it may appear, however jealous he might be of him, or disposed to charge him with faults of which he was not guilty, the property he had

for years been amassing he had intended for
him and him alone.

Had Philip lived a few years longer the case
might have been different, though he had never,
even when the youth was in high favour, intended
to leave anything entirely in his own hands.

'He must,' he thought, 'get a cooler head
before he gets any of my money. He would
spend it a hundred times faster than I have
been able to collect it. His father is a conceited, soft-headed fellow, but he knows the
value of money, and I can trust him with mine
when I am gone.' But now he thought, as he
sat alone in his easy-chair after his master had
left him,—'What is to be done now? I never
dreamed he would go first, though I often told
him perhaps he would. Well, I must take care
I am not robbed now, and keep what I have
for myself. I may retire and get married again,
as I have sometimes thought of doing. I am
only eighty-three, and I have known men less
sound than I am live till they were a hundred
years old, and I have heard of others nearly up
to one hundred and twenty; and why should
not I? I am hale and hearty, and if it was
not for a twitch I get now and then of lumbago
and gout, I should be well enough all round to
live as long as any one.' So the old man

thought and murmured on, with as little sympathy for others as he had excess of regard for himself.

Very different was the spirit that held possession of the drawing-room in the Hall that evening. Tears were not wanting to make the sorrowful feeling evident that held the mastery there. True, it was but a servant that was gone ; and were there not abundance of others ready to fill his place ? So many an one would have argued, but so did not Sir Edward. He declared that he had not only lost an invaluable servant, but a humble friend, upon whose fidelity and faithfulness he could at all times and in all places put his most unlimited trust.

But the young people looked upon him as one of themselves. From the first day they could be trusted with their feet to the ground, many a romp and scramble had they, from the youngest to the eldest, had together with him ; yet never had he before strangers failed to treat them with the respect and deference due to their station. Whether the knowledge he had that his services were valued and appreciated had any part in producing that respect for their position may be matter for argument ; but of the reality of the kind feeling that existed on both sides there can be no doubt.

During the greater part of the evening Sir Edward and Mr Gordon sat apart, conversing in low tones, while the young people drew their chairs together to talk and comment in subdued whispers on the events of the day. Of course the name of Dixon was not forgotten.

'I cannot understand,' said Grace, 'why they kept Dixon in prison if he was not guilty.'

'Because the circumstances of the case were not fully known until they came out before the grand jury to-day,' observed Charlotte.

'And what is a grand jury?' asked Grace. 'I get from one puzzle to another, and the last is the hardest.'

'The grand jury,' replied Charlotte, 'is, I believe, formed of a number of magistrates or other gentlemen, who, before a charge against a prisoner is sent up to the judge, go over the evidence that is to be produced, and determine its character.'

'Then I suppose they were not satisfied with it in Dixon's case?' observed Oliver.

'What are you saying about Dixon?' asked Sir Edward.

'We were talking of the reason of his being set at liberty,' replied Grace.

'I think,' observed Sir Edward, 'we shall be doing no more than may fairly be expected of us if we send for him to come up to us this evening, that we may congratulate him on his escape from further punishment for his sup-posed crime. I can answer for myself that I feel I ought to do so, for I must confess that till last night I thought there was a great probability that he fired the fatal shot.'

'Did you, indeed, papa,' said Grace; 'you never told us so before.'

'No,' replied Sir Edward; 'I should have done wrong if I had told you what I thought.'

'But, I said, I thought he was not guilty,' said Grace. 'Was that wrong? If it was, Jesse did wrong too; for he said he was quite sure he was innocent.'

'It might not be wrong for you or Jesse,' replied her father; 'but you see, Grace, our positions are not just alike in the world, and therefore our responsibilities are not the same. You have written to Jesse, as I directed you?' he added to Oliver.

'Yes, papa,' replied Oliver, 'I wrote to him immediately on our return home.'

'That is well,' said his father; 'and now we will send for Dixon.'

'Poor fellow,' said Mr Gordon; 'it must be a great comfort to him to know that his mother has not been in want during his confinement.'

'Jesse must be thanked for that, I think,' said Charlotte.

'I have sent for you, Dixon,' said Sir Edward, when the man entered the room, 'that you may hear from my lips how very sorry I am for the unfortunate mistake which caused you to be sent to prison.'

'Thank you, Sir Edward,' said Dixon.

'I suppose you do not wish to leave my service?'

'No, Sir Edward; I shall be glad to go back to my old work again, and I hope I shall be able to let you see how thankful I am for your kindness to my mother when I was not able to help her.'

'Much of your trouble,' said Sir Edward, 'arose from the hasty words you were reported to have indulged in against the unfortunate youth who was so suddenly taken from us; I trust you will be more guarded in future.'

'I will try,' Sir Edward.

'And pray to God to help you, then you will doubtless make a good use of your recovered liberty, and be a comfort to your mother as long as she lives.'

Though we have for some time lost sight of Jasper, he has on that account been a not

less prominent agent in his little world than
heretofore. It was observed that when he
became too talkative of what was taking place,
and his master was obliged to shun him, that
he betook himself to an old crony, where he
could talk to his heart's content without fear
of interruption.

Now this old crony was a dame who lived
at a cottage at the extreme end of the village,
and made herself useful in the world by acting
as carrier between the village and a market-
town about five miles distant. She had a small
horse, very poorly kept, and a cart that made
when in motion a rattling noise that gave notice
of her approach long before she came in sight.

She had passed her seventieth year, and was
a little deaf, and not quite so clear-eyed as she
had been a few years since, and without either
husband or son to help her along the rough
road of life. Of her three daughters, the only
children her husband had left her, two were
married and had left the village. The third,
not quite a child, having added nearly forty
years to her birth date, was at home with her
mother assisting in the household work, groom-
ing the horse, and doing any odd jobs, as she
said, that came in her way.

When their day's work was over, they would

welcome Jasper to their cottage, and sit down with him by the fire, with their ears as wide open as they could get them, to listen to the little budget of news he had to bring them from the Hall. The old dame would ever and anon make some shrewd remark in answer to what he had said; but, owing to her defective hearing power, it often went wide of its purpose.

But while Jasper only gossiped with the mother, he captivated the daughter.

Her head was reported to be of the softest character, and by the furtive glance with which she regarded her visitor when she was not looking directly and lovingly into his face, it might very safely be supposed that her heart acted in pleasant unison with it, so that between the two no disagreement could ever take place to the injury of either.

When Jasper opened his battery of censure upon the coroner and jury for having sent Dixon to prison, he became a greater man than ever in their eyes. The mother was pleased because, in his anger, he spoke so loud that she could hear him without difficulty, and the daughter delighted because he spoke out so bravely for a poor fellow who, as she agreed, was unjustly shut up, and could not speak for himself.

Nancy was the daughter's name, and it was not long before Jasper discovered that Nancy's attention to him was daily on the increase, which caused him to think a little seriously of making his visits less frequent. But, as fate would have it, things had arrived just at this point when Oliver, in obedience to his father's request, told Jasper that he thought he was getting too old, and too much of a man, to continue longer in his present place.

'I am quite content to stop with you, sir,' said Jasper.

'Would you not like a better situation?'

'No, I don't want one,' said Jasper, very eagerly; 'where should I get such another master as you are?'

'Oh, you will soon get one quite as good, or better.'

'I don't know where, sir,' said Jasper, very dolefully. 'Besides I don't want to leave you; but if you say I must go, I suppose I must.'

'I do not say you must,' said Oliver, 'but I want you to think whether it would not be better for you.'

'Well, I will think about it,' said Jasper; 'but I am pretty sure, unless something very particular should happen, there will be no change of mind for me.'

That evening he related the circumstance to Nancy and her mother, when an idea flashed across the soft brain of the former, which, in due time, wrought an alteration in her position, the particulars of which the reader may discover in another chapter.

CHAPTER VI.

THE change of mind respecting the time of his return home from Brighton was a very sudden affair with Jesse. He had gone out to the beach to cool his brain with the sea air, or rather with the hope of doing so, as it was not the first time he had tried its effects, and feeling no benefit from it had returned back to his room at the hotel, murmuring to himself, 'I believe I am growing more stupid every day.'

Falling back upon the natural energy of his character, he had often endeavoured to persuade himself that he was quite well and able for any amount of work if he were to return home. But it was to no purpose, and after a slight struggle he soon found himself sinking again into a state of listless apathy, that made him careless of what he did, or where he went. Then he would exclaim, 'What a fool I am that I cannot shake off this detestable feeling. While the world is all bustle and life around me, I am nowhere. I cannot form a resolution and hold to it, even for five minutes together, without a change.'

Poor Jesse, he was in the midst of the trial which at one period or another falls to the lot of most young people, and from which their elders are not at all times entirely free. There was a void place in his heart that mere fancy could not fill, though the ideal form of a certain person crossed and recrossed his brain in a most lively fashion, sometimes, apparently, without any reference to his own will.

' I am so stupid,' he thought, after wandering about on the beach for some time, ' that I could for very vexation throw myself into the sea, and make an end of it. But to drown oneself from the beach at Brighton could not be seriously thought of.' From some point in one of the piers the business might be accomplished ; so on to the old pier he went, not however fully intent on committing suicide, but just to learn if a man might go over the rails into the water without a chance of being ignobly pulled out again, and taken before the mayor and charged with attempting to commit a crime which only a fool could be guilty of, unless he was in a state of absolute insanity.

'It would be easy enough no doubt,' he thought, 'for a man to jump into the sea, but there could be but little hope of his being left there. Some one would be soon at hand hauling him unceremoniously into a boat by the head or heels, or any other part that might come more readily to his grasp. No, such an escape from his languor was not to be attempted at Brighton in the open day, either from the beach or pier.'

While he stood leaning over the rails dreaming of nothing, as he would at another time have laughingly said, a sailing boat, with two or three men in it, arrested his attention. 'My fine fellows,' he thought, 'you are carrying too much sail for your little craft, and are in a fair way of discovering for yourselves a taste of the sea. Now, if one were with you, there might be a chance of getting drowned by accident, as it would be called, if you are, as I suspect you will be very soon, capsized.' Then he cried, as he saw her sails nearly touch the water, 'If you do not shorten sail you will go to the bottom!'

'All right, sir,' called out a voice from the

boat, ' we are not for the fishes yet,' and away
they sped on their mad career.

' Have you room for a passenger?' shouted
Jesse, with the desperate intention of going to
the bottom with them, but his voice did not
reach the men in the boat, or was not heeded
by them, as they sailed away out into the open
sea.

As listlessly as he had strolled on to the pier
so listlessly did Jesse commence his return to
the shore, when, at a few paces from him, his
eyes fell upon an advancing figure, that caused
him to rub them with doubt and astonishment,
to discover whether it was really Miss Montag,
with her little charge, he saw, or whether it was
an unsubstantial shape, the work of his wayward
imagination.

The question was soon solved, it was Lizzie
herself with Georgie Smith. The meeting was
a mutual surprise. What might come of it
they did not stop to inquire, but its immediate
effect upon them was too apparent for mistake.
At the moment their hands were clasped together, their eyes met, and told each other of
the all-pervading love that filled their hearts.

Had they met, as of old, in the shady walks
or green fields of the country, they would
doubtless have been more guarded in the

expressions that broke almost involuntarily from their lips. From that moment they were in loving communion with each other. No protestations of love were necessary. No, nor even its name in words. The mutual expression of their eyes told them of the strong bond of sympathetic feeling that existed between their hearts.

'Why, Miss Montag,' exclaimed Jesse, as he seized her hand and pressed it warmly in his own, 'you are one of the last persons I expected or hoped to meet here!'

'I have been in Brighton for nearly three weeks,' replied Miss Montag, with her face at first deadly pale, then suddenly flushing crimson.

'For three weeks!' echoed Jesse, 'Why, I have been here for several days myself. How is it that we have not met before? I have certainly not seen you, and I very much hope you have not seen me.'

'I think I have seen you in the distance,' replied Miss Montag timidly, but she did not say she had purposely kept out of his sight, because she could not meet him as a friend, and would not meet him as a stranger. She knew but too well of the yearning of her heart towards him, but she also knew how hopeless its indulgence would be, and therefore resolved if possible not to meet him.

'You think you saw me,' said Jesse. 'Why then did you not come and speak to me, as I would have done to you had the chance been mine?'

The child who had been a little frightened by the sudden approach of Jesse, and his eagerly taking the hand of his protectress, soon discovered that the new comer was not an enemy but an old friend.

'Ah!' he stammered, as he looked up with beseeching eyes, 'you not speak to Georgie?'

'My poor little fellow,' cried Jesse, as he caught him up in his arms, and kissed him, 'I am very glad to see you here, and so far recovered. Good Miss Montag has taken great care of you.'

'And Georgie good too,' said the child.

'Oh yes, always,' said Jesse, as he restored him to his feet.

'You have not told me,' he continued, taking up the thread of his discourse at the point where it had been broken in upon by the child, 'why you left me in ignorance of your presence here?'

'Please do not press me for an answer,' she murmured.

' I will not,' said Jesse, in a tremulous voice,
' if it points to a secret you wish to keep from
me ? '

' I can have no secrets I wish to keep from
you.'

' Then I must press for an answer to my
question.'

' Pray, do not.'

' Yes, I must,' said Jesse.

Seeing there was no escape from her dilemma
but by speaking the truth, or equivocating,
which might lead to an unfortunate misunderstanding, she said, ' I thought it would not be
considered proper that I should make advances
to you in the public streets of Brighton.'

' Advances,' said Jesse, ' who will say that
speaking to an old friend, when you meet one,
is making improper advances.'

' Our positions in the world are so different,'
she murmured.

Jesse considered for a moment and then said,
' I see you would remind me that I am
the son of a baronet, and that you are below
me in station. Now, pray let me tell you once
for all, that such a consideration does not
weigh in my mind the shadow of a scruple
as far as I am concerned. But if it has any
allusion to your own reputation, that is an

entirely different thing, and ·I am bound to attend to it.'

'I was not thinking of myself.'

'Then think no more of· it,' said Jesse eagerly. 'It is true, I am not in the eyes of the world my own master, but I think I am of my own heart, and that heart Miss Montag—'

'Pray, let us talk of something else?' she said, interrupting him, and trembling with agitation.

'No,' said Jesse, 'we will not, until I have told you all. Our meeting here this morning has been accidental, and I am now perhaps surprised into a confession that my heart, with all its best affections, is entirely yours, and has been so for a very long time. Let that suffice on my part. Now, what have you to say on yours?'

'That I now more than ever,' replied Miss Montag sorrowfully, 'mourn over my ignorance of my birth, and of the position my parents occupied in the world.'

'But what can that have to do with my question?'

'Your father loves you as his own soul,' rejoined the now excited girl, 'and what would he do if you were to tell him what you have just declared to me?'

'Well, I dare say,' rejoined Jesse, 'he would be a little startled at first, but he is a just and reasonable man, and would not bid me die.'

'Die!' echoed the alarmed girl.

'Yes—die,' repeated Jesse; 'for, deprived of you, what should I have to live for? Say, can you not trust your heart with me, assured of its safe keeping. I will not ask you to do anything rash, nor will I, if I can help it, act rashly myself. In a few days I shall return home and speak to my father.'

'And you will be guided by him?' she said nervously.

'Yes, entirely, if possible,' was the quick reply; 'for I know he will not ask me to do anything that is not right.' Then looking earnestly at her, he added, 'You are satisfied now, and can give me a favourable answer.'

'What can I say more than you know?'

'Then you confess your heart is mine?' said Jesse.

'Yes,' she murmured; 'but I am afraid I am doing wrong.'

Jesse, beside himself with joy, would have clasped her in his arms, and sworn eternal fidelity to her, but the old pier at Brighton was not exactly the place for such a display to pass unnoticed, and if it had been, that was, as it proved, not the time for it. The boy, who had been running up and down and around them, suddenly stumbled and fell forward on his face. He was not very much hurt, though he made a good use of his lungs to call attention to his mishap, when Miss Montag, self-condemned for her want of care, caught him up in her arms and covered him with kisses.

'You kiss Georgie, too,' said the child, with tearful eyes, to Jesse.

Jesse, nothing loath, as his lips would follow where Miss Montag's had so lately been, did his work so heartily that the child put up his little hand to push him away as he said,—

'Go away; hurt Georgie.'

It was a curious coincidence, though perhaps not so very curious as it might at first sight appear, that at the identical time when the love scene on the pier at Brighton was taking place, a little bird was whispering in the ear of Mrs Smith that Mr Jesse Harewood was gone to Brighton for the benefit of the sea air.

'Gone to Brighton! Well, now, that is droll—that is where Smith's brother lives.'

She said no more to the little bird, but she told her husband directly he came in that

she was quite longing to see her Georgie
again, and that she thought he had been
away long enough now.

'Send to Miss Montag to bring him home
then,' said Smith. 'It isn't a matter that
seems to want much talking about.'

'Shall I write at once and tell her to bring
him home to-morrow, or perhaps you will
write to your brother and ask him to tell
her?'

'No, I shall have nothing to do with it,'
said Smith. 'You settled about the going,
and you must do the same about the coming
back.'

Miss Montag was surprised at her sudden
recall, but she was not very sorry to leave
Brighton. She felt that she was living in
an uncomfortable state of happiness, if such
an expression is admissible. If she stopped
there she knew that she would be frequently
meeting with Jesse, and receiving his attention
with unmixed pleasure, but until he had spoken
to his father, she feared to trust unreservedly
in the bright prospect before her, lest some
bitter disappointment should come upon
them.

When Jesse heard of the order for the
return, he flushed up, and said she could not

go so soon. It was unreasonable on the part of Mrs Smith to expect she could.

'You must stop here for another week at the very least,' he said; 'and, if you like, I will write and tell her so.'

'That would not be wise,' replied Miss Montag, 'I am afraid. Perhaps even Mrs Smith would not approve of your interesting yourself about me.'

'Then I will go up with you,' said Jesse, in a decided tone.

'I should be sorry to say anything in opposition to what you may think right, but it surely would be better for me to go alone.'

'I cannot see it so,' said Jesse.

'You would not wish a whisper to reach your father's ears of our having met and been seen together here, much less our travelling home in the same carriage?'

'I would rather speak to him first,' said Jesse; 'though I do not care a straw who talks of having seen us together here. You are not afraid of Brighton gossip, are you?'

'No,' replied Miss Montag; 'but I would give as little occasion for it as possible. Just let me go in accordance with Mrs Smith's wish, and then you can follow in the course of two or three days.'

' Two or three days,' said Jesse. 'And what am I to do with myself here all that time ? I shall be as dull and miserable as ever.'

But he could not refute the reasons she gave for doing as she proposed, though he would not agree with them.

The next morning found him no better pleased to be left behind, and it was with anything but a smiling face that he met Miss Montag at the station, and saw her and her charge safely off in the train.

Since his meeting with his adventure on the pier, he had in a wonderful manner recovered his spirits, but as he turned from the station he felt them sink within him, and a throbbing pain shot across his temples, reminding him too surely that the Brighton air was not an all sufficient remedy for his diseased brain.

' I will write at once to my father,' he thought, 'and tell him that I have no chance of getting well here, and that he may expect to see me home to-morrow.'

In so great a hurry was he to accomplish his purpose that, instead of going up to his room to his well-stocked desk of pen, ink, and paper, he entered the coffee-room, and, knowing he should find materials for writing there, sat down and prepared to commence his task.

There were several gentlemen in the room, and before he had got the date on the paper his attention was arrested by two who sat near him.

It so happened that it was the day following the one on which Dixon had regained his liberty. Owing to Miss Montag's departure Jesse had not seen the morning papers, nor received Oliver's letter, which was lying un-opened in his room upstairs.

'This Woodfield business seems to have been strangely managed,' said one of the gentlemen to his friend.

'I do not know to what you allude,' was the reply.

'You have not seen the paper?'

'Yes, I have, but I saw nothing of Wood-field.'

'Look at that, then, and tell me if you do not think there is something wrong in our laws, when a man can be shut up for days or weeks on the bare suspicion that he is guilty of a crime which has never been committed, and of which he is consequently entirely in-nocent.'

'It appears rather hard upon the man Dixon,' said the gentleman, who had been running his eye over the paper while the other was speaking.

These few words told Jesse that Dixon had not been found guilty. He dropped his pen and took up a paper to assure himself of the particulars of the trial. As he did so his eyes rested for a moment on the speakers. He saw they were two elderly gentlemen, one of whom bore on his features unmistakable evidence of his having spent much of his time in a foreign country. The other looking nothing different from a stay-at-home Englishman.

Jesse set to work on his paper, and, under ordinary circumstances, would have paid no more attention to them, but he had scanned only a few lines when his eyes ceased to convey to his brain the matter before him, and gave up their office to his ears.

'Woodcome Hall is in the parish of Woodfield, is it not?' said the foreign-looking gentleman, Mr Anson, to his friend.

'Yes,' replied his friend, Mr Horn; 'and I have heard that it was a lucky chance for the present proprietor that placed it in his hands. The late Sir Henry spent much of his time on the Continent, where, I think, I heard you incidentally say you met him.'

'I saw him frequently at one period of his life,' said Mr Anson; 'he came to me for advice.'

'He was spoken of in London as being a very free liver,' said Mr Horn.

'Free,' rejoined Mr Anson. 'Yes, and if I were to tell you only a part of his proceedings you might have good reason to think I was composing a romance.'

'Did he gamble?'

'Yes, to the extent of his means, and, I suspect, sometimes beyond them; but gambling was not his strong point. Think of rich dinners, good wine, and women, and you will be nearer the mark.'

'But he had a wife,' said Mr Horn.

'Comparatively speaking, only for a short time,' rejoined Mr Anson. 'His married life did not commence until he had passed his fortieth year, and it was finished in his fiftieth, and, if the reports current at the time were to be trusted, he would not have taken a wife then if an increase of fortune had not made the sacrifice of his liberty necessary. She bore him but one child — a son, who, after her death, spent too much of his time in his father's company. He proved to be a clever youth, but he was too readily influenced by the unthinking men that he gathered around him.'

'Surely his father did not take him into his society.'

'Well, not exactly, but so near to it that it was not possible for him to escape suffering from its influence. For awhile, after being withdrawn from college, he had a tutor or travelling companion to accompany him ; but that, I believe, did not last long, so that, at an early age, the youth became virtually his own master, with his father's purse open to his hand.

'The training of the youth soon brought forth its fruit. Before he was nineteen he had entangled himself in a real or sham marriage, with a young lady in reduced circumstances. This he had contrived by the aid of an old servant, while his father was away on a visit to some friends in Switzerland.

'The young lady was an orphan, but not absolutely friendless. Her protector, however, was only an old aunt, who lived in a small house, and had as much as she could do to meet her weekly expenses. The old servant, feeling the youth was, to some extent, under his charge, and seeing that, if he could not obtain the girl by any other means, he would marry her, and thereby incur for them both the displeasure of Sir Henry. The man knew that, whatever might be said to the son, he would never be forgiven if he suffered such a thing to take place; and if, on the other hand, he sent an account of what he feared to his master, he would incur the hatred of the youth, and perchance bring about an exposure of certain intrigues in which they had both been engaged.'

Thus far Jesse had heard tolerably well the account of the late Sir Henry Harewood and his son, which Mr Anson was giving to his friend; but here, much to his annoyance, a break occurred in the narrative, through the entrance of some more gentlemen, who, sitting down near the two friends, caused their conversation to be carried on in a lower tone, so that Jesse could only catch here and there a word of what was passing between them. He could only gather that some kind of marriage had taken place. That two children had been born, and he thought he could make out they were twins; but what became of them or their mother he could not understand.

While the conversation was going on Jesse sat with the newspaper before his face. He would not have sought to play the eavesdropper, but the words that met his ear were too interesting to cause him to think he was doing wrong by listening to them.

The gentlemen having finished their bottle of wine, rose from their chairs; Jesse immediately did the same, with the impulse strong upon him of at once introducing himself to them, to obtain their names and address for further inquiry into a matter which so nearly concerned his family. But he desisted from his purpose when he remembered that he was in a public room; and his speaking to them there might lead to a misunderstanding, and end in confusion.

Then he reseated himself, and took up his paper again, and learnt all it could tell him of the expected trial and the liberation of Dixon. Seeing a waiter near, he asked him who the two gentlemen were who had been sitting near him, and who had just left the room.

'I don't know, sir, but I will inquire,' said the man.

In a few seconds he returned, and said they were strangers at the hotel.

'Have they engaged rooms?' asked Jesse.

'No, sir; they said their luggage was at the station, and they were going from Brighton by the next train.'

'When does the train leave?'

'I think it is on the point of starting now,

sir. The omnibus left the door some minutes since.'

Jesse stayed for no further question, but rushing from the door of the hotel, jumped into a fly, calling out to the driver as he did so,—

' To the station as quick as you can go !'

' Which one, sir ?' inquired the driver.

' The one the omnibus has just gone to.'

' All right, sir,' cried the driver, and off they went at an extra shilling rate. They had not, however, gone many yards when they were met by two youths riding on bicycles, who seemed a little nervous at the sudden appearance of the fly, and not able at the moment to decide how to keep out of its way. This resulted in the driver pulling his horse aside with so much force that the poor beast, after struggling forward a few steps, fell heavily to the ground.

' All right, sir !' cried the driver, as he jumped from the box. ' Keep your seat, sir. Up in a minute.'

At the end of five minutes Jesse's stock of patience was exhausted. He sprang from his seat, and calling out, ' Come to the hotel for your fare,' started off towards the station like a madman.

Again vexatious disappointment awaited him.

He reached a station, but only to find it was the wrong one. Then, without a moment's delay, he was off for the other, but though he made use of another fly which went at a good rate without meeting with any accident, he only reached the entrance just in time to see the end of the train in the distance hurrying along on the rails after the engine.

By this time Jesse was fully aroused from his lethargy, and he, to the no small astonishment of the bystanders, wished all the bicycles at the bottom of the sea. Seeing that a little crowd was gathering around him, he said, ' Two of those stupid two-wheeled things threw my horse down, and made me lose the train.'

'Why, your horse seemed all right enough when you came in sight,' said some of the crowd.

' I do not mean that one,' cried Jesse, as he entered the booking-office. ' It was the other.'

Then he knocked lustily with his knuckles at the little door of the money-taker, and as it was thrown back with an angry jerk, asked hurriedly if two gentlemen had just taken tickets for London, one with a foreign look, and the other rather pale.

'Perhaps they have,' was the reply, ' but we have no time to look at passengers' faces when they are pressing one upon the other for tickets. But if they did, they are gone to London, as the train does not stop till it gets there.' And the little door jumped back again into its place.

'Not over civil,' thought Jesse, as he turned away, on his return to the hotel. Arrived there, he passed at once to his room, where he found Oliver's letter, which took his mind from his late exciting chase and its cause to his friends at home, and the more than ordinary incident that had lately occurred there.

Having mastered the contents of his letter, and written his reply, he threw himself into an arm-chair to consider where he was, what he had done, and what he had to do.

CHAPTER VII.

WHILE Jesse was being aroused from his lethargy at Brighton, and hopefully looking forward to happier days, a cloud was gathering at Downend which threatened ere long to bring a tempest of no common character upon Elston Court, if a change in the state of affairs did not shortly intervene, and scatter its darkening influence.

It was but the old story renewed. Another letter had reached Mr Cresswell from his friend at Marseilles, by which he learnt that the money he had sent for Lyson had been handed to him, but his friend had good reason to believe that it had been misapplied. The tourist party, according to Lyson, had through some misunderstanding respecting the time of starting, left the harbour without him, and carried off with them his luggage and the greater part of his available cash.

As a matter of course, another letter quickly followed this, in which his friend stated that Lyson had just called upon him again with a pitiful tale of his being in extreme want of money, and begging for another advance on Mr Cresswell's account. 'I informed Mr Lyson,' wrote his friend, 'that I had no authority from you to comply with his request, when he said angrily that if I would not assist him out of his difficulty he should be tempted to do something that his friends would be sorry to hear of; whereupon I told him I would have nothing more to do with him or his difficulties, and that if he had any communication he wished to make to you he was of all persons in the world the most fitting to do it.

'In dealing thus with your son-in-law,' said the writer, 'I trust you will not think I have acted disrespectfully towards you, for had I felt that he needed the money for any legitimate purpose I would have instantly let him have it without any scruple respecting your approval of the action. I do not think he will trouble me again, but if he does I shall only repeat what I have already told him; and if I might venture to offer you a little friendly advice, I would say do not, if he should write to you, believe too readily any statement he may make to you, either of what I have done or refused to do, or his account of the poverty into which the actions of false friends have plunged him.'

The letter containing this unpleasant intelligence unfortunately fell into the hands of Edith and her mother. And this was the manner of its doing so. Mr Cresswell received it when engaged in writing a letter in his library ; the servant who brought it, knowing that he need not wait for an answer, placed it without a word on the table and left the room. Having finished the sentence he was writing, Mr Cresswell turned to the letter, and observing that it was from the Continent, immediately opened it and made himself acquainted with its contents. Then he sank back in his chair, murmuring as he did so, 'Will this man never cease to be a thorn in my side ?'

After sitting thoughtful and silent for some time, he decided that he would ride over to Woodfield, and once more lay the troublesome affair before Sir Edward, and see if he could advise him how to proceed to put a stop to the annoyance to which he had so long been a martyr. But that he might not come to a hasty conclusion he re-read the letter, and then putting it down again, proceeded to finish the one upon which he was engaged, when the servant entered the room.

Having completed his task he drew his loose papers with a trembling hand into the drawer, and, as he did so, accidentally brushed off the important letter he had just received into the waste-paper basket. Rising from his seat he placed the empty envelope in his breast-pocket, and left the room to tell his wife that, as the morning was very fine, and he had not had much exercise lately, he thought he would ride over to Woodfield.

' You will have the carriage, papa, will you not ? ' asked Edith, who happened to be in the room with her mother.

' Yes, I think so,' was the reply.

' Then, if you will take us with you, we shall be pleased to accompany you.'

As their presence was the very thing he wished to avoid, he walked to the window without appearing to hear what his daughter had said.

' No, not the carriage,' he added half aloud. It is very fine, and a brisk ride on my cob will do me good.'

' I was saying, papa,' urged Edith, ' that if you were going in the carriage—'

' No,' said her father interrupting her, ' I shall ride over on horseback.'

'I am rather pleased to hear you say so,' interposed Mrs Cresswell, 'as I do not feel equal for much visiting to-day, and I know Edith would not like to go without me.'

'I shall not be late from home,' observed Mr Cresswell, as he left the room to prepare for his little journey.

'Oh dear,' said Edith, 'I am afraid papa has had some unpleasant news by the post; he seemed so very cheerful at breakfast time, but now he has that old anxious look that I am so sorry to see on his features; and you too are not well.'

'You trouble yourself too much about us,' said her mother, 'and do you know I some-times think you forget we are getting old.'

'Oh no, mamma,' rejoined Edith with a smile, 'I cannot forget that, seeing how old I am growing myself.'

As soon as the sound of the hoofs of the horse on which Mr Cresswell was riding had died away in the distance, Edith, as was her custom, went into the library to put in order any papers and books her father might have left scattered about. Like most gentlemen, he had a great dislike to a servant being suffered, duster in hand, to go into his room in his absence with her untutored notions of making everything clean and comfortable. Edith had long since discovered the state of his mind in that particular, and had taken upon herself the task of doing all that was necessary to be done from day to day in the library, excepting the fireplace and the carpet, when the open book-case was covered up for a general sweep.

The waste-paper basket came in for a share of her attention. More than once she had recovered papers from it that had slipped in without notice, and whose loss might have occasioned some trouble. On these irregularities being discovered, it was her practice to put the papers in a place of safety, and report the fact as of no account to her father.

Thus it was that, without any undue curiosity on her part, the important letter from Marseilles fell into her hands. As might have been expected, its contents threw her into a state of great excitement. For some time she had heard no particulars of her husband, and she was under the impression her father knew no more of him than she did. Now she was suddenly undeceived. Not only had her father known of his whereabouts, but she could perceive that he had been, indirectly at least, in correspondence with him.

She stood with the letter considering how she ought to act, when the door opened and her mother entered the room. This had the effect of increasing her excitement; what should she do? Should she tell her mother of the discovery she had made, and make her as wretched as herself? She stood irresolute, not knowing what to say or do.

'Why, Edith,' said her mother, 'what ails you? You look as if you had suddenly come upon a gunpowder plot, or something quite as startling.'

'I have found something that has greatly surprised me, mother,' stammered Edith.

'You have not been reading your father's letters, I hope?' said her mother.

'I have read nothing but what I found in the waste-paper basket,' said Edith.

'Oh, then,' said Mrs Cresswell, greatly relieved, 'it cannot be of much consequence.'

'No, certainly,' replied Edith; 'so I will just put it aside, and say no more about it.'

'I suppose its proper place is the basket,' said Mrs Cresswell. 'Your father would not have put it there if it had been of any consequence, unless, indeed,' she added after a slight pause, 'he wished you to see it.'

'Wished me to see it, mother!' repeated Edith,

and as she spoke a new light appeared to break in upon her mind.

'Was it possible,' she asked herself, 'that her father wished her to know what was taking place, and had not the heart to speak to her before she had in some measure become acquainted with it? Yes, it must be so,' she concluded, and then continued aloud,—

'And now, what is to be done? Shall I tell my father immediately on his return, or wait for him to allude to it?'

'You forget,' said her mother, 'that I do not know to what you expect he will allude. I have not seen the letter.'

'If my father intended me to see it,' said Edith, 'he could not object to my showing it to you.'

'This is very unfortunate,' said Mrs Cresswell, when she had made herself acquainted with the contents of the letter. 'Yes, it is most unfortunate,' she repeated; 'and I am very sorry, Edith, that you have read it.'

'But if my father left it on the top of his basket that I should read—'

'There must have been some mistake for it to get there,' said Mrs Cresswell, interrupting her daughter. 'I know your father too well to imagine for a moment that he would adopt such an indirect method of making you acquainted with anything he wished you to know.'

While she was speaking, she saw from the window a horseman coming rapidly towards the house. The letter dropped from her trembling hand, as she said,—

'It is your father coming back. Now you will soon know if he intended you to see it. Put the letter back in the place where you took it from, until we discover why he has returned so soon.'

'Ah!' said Mr Cresswell as he entered the room, 'my little maid has lost no time in getting to work in my absence. You are surprised to see me back so soon, but I am not come to stop. I very carelessly left a paper behind which I wished to show to Sir Edward.' As he spoke he went to his table-drawer and unlocked it, and began hastily to search among its contents, continuing as he did so,—'It was by the merest chance I discovered my mistake. Plague take the paper!' he cried. 'Where can it be? I certainly had it by me when I was writing. Could I have dropped it into the basket?' When he turned to that all further search was unnecessary. There lay the letter uncovered before his eye. Eagerly he seized

it, put it in his pocket, and was about to leave
the room, when Mrs Cresswell said,—

' What! going without one word to the poor
old wife ? '

' I have lost so much time by my stupid
blunder,' he replied, ' that I must beg you to
excuse my seeming neglect.'

As he spoke his eyes glanced from his wife
to his daughter, and in a moment he became
aware that something unusual had occurred
during his brief absence. There was an anxious,
inquiring look upon their features that told him
as plainly as a loving whisper would have done
had it sounded in his ears,—' We know all ; can
you not trust us ? ' ' If they have seen the letter,'
he thought, ' further attempt at disguise on my
part will be useless.'

Edith, seeing his perplexing hesitation and
guessing its cause, went quietly up to him, and
putting her hand gently on his arm, said,—

' Father, I have seen the letter.'

' If you have read it, you have done very
wrong,' he replied. ' You must have known the
instant you saw it that I did not put it there for
you to read.'

' When I first took it in my hand,' said
Edith, ' I thought it was waste paper, and
merely looked at it, not, as you may suppose,

out of curiosity, but really to see if I thought
you intended it to be destroyed, as I have done
by your loose papers many times before. Having commenced to read it, I could not stop
until I reached the end. If I have done wrong,
I must beg you to pardon me. My punishment
will be more than sufficient to know that I have
offended and grieved you.'

'My poor child,' said Mr Cresswell, 'if I am
angry or grieved, it is not for what you have
done, but with myself, for my own fault in leaving it so carelessly for you to see. You do not
know how incessantly I have striven for months
past to keep all this and the like unfortunate
business from you.'

'I am sorry, very sorry,' rejoined Edith,
'that I have been the cause of so much trouble
to you.'

'I spoke not in the way of complaint,' said
her father, 'but simply to let you know how
very sorry I am that all my caution has been to
no purpose, through my own carelessness. For
you, I think you must know that you have my
warmest sympathy and most sincere pity.'

'Then please take me fully into your confidence, and let me show you that I am not un-
deserving of your sympathy and pity, and my
mother too. Be sure that in this matter you

can trust us. Why should you keep all this trouble to yourself, when it is not of your own creating, and you have us to share it with you ?'

'This was the business that was taking you to Woodfield?' said Mrs Cresswell.

'Yes,' replied her husband; 'but since you have broken in upon my secret, when I return I will make amends for my past silence by answering as fully as I can every question you may put to me.'

In a few minutes Mr Cresswell was again on the road for Woodfield, and his wife and daughter sitting down conversing together in subdued tones of what the unseen future might have in store for them.

The result of Mr Cresswell's consultation with Sir Edward Harewood at Woodfield, and with his wife and daughter on his return home, was expressed in a letter he sent to his friend at Marseilles, in which he spoke of the great obligation he felt he was under to him, and how highly he approved of his determination to have nothing further to do with a man who had shown so little regard for truth and honesty.

'If you chance to meet with him again,' he continued, 'and he persists in annoying you, pray let me hear from you again, and I will write to him, and if possible bring him to a sense of his misconduct. You may rest assured he will have my opinion very plainly expressed of the light in which I view his mean actions and despicable schemes. Should you hear any idle reports he may set abroad of my harsh dealing with him, you will add to the debt I owe you by treating the matter with contempt.'

So for the time the matter ended. Mr Cresswell did not make any report of it to Mr Lyson, who was every day growing more complaining and childish, nor to the sisters of the profligate, as he knew it would only lead them to utter a multitude of words to no purpose, to show how much their dear brother was to be pitied.

Sir Edward was equally silent with his friends. He had great confidence in Mr Gordon; but this he looked upon as a family matter, in which a stranger could not be well called upon to give advice. As for his daughters, the whole affair was of too delicate a nature to be brought before them in any shape whatever.

To Oliver he could not speak with any hope of being understood; and as it occurred while

Jesse was at Brighton, he must perforce remain ignorant of what was taking place.

Had Sir Edward known the cause of Jesse's proposal to return home, he would have had but little reason to be pleased; but in his ignorance of that he was delighted with the cheerful tone of his last letter, in which he said he was feeling quite well, and he had good hope that it would be a very long time before he had one of his old dull, mopish fits again.

To Oliver the news of his brother's return was most welcome. Though he had some reason to be jealous of him, not a spark of it had ever entered his head or heart. Compared with himself, he looked upon his brother almost as a being of another world. He had no more idea now, than when he was an infant, how Jesse could stand up in the midst of a room full of company, and give his opinion on any matter in question, without a tremor in his voice or nervous twitching in his face.

They were always the best of friends; he was confiding, and Jesse was generous, with no desire to set off his ability at the expense of his brother.

Oliver was a little perplexed after hearing of Jesse's return, to know how he should manage with his sister Charlotte and Miss Gordon. It had become part of the business of the day with him to go with them on their visits to the school, and on their rounds of mercy to the poor and afflicted of the parish. He carried the basket containing all the necessary things for the missionary of a parish, when assisted and smiled upon by a rich and powerful neighbour.

There was meat for the convalescent, jelly for the sick, soft bread for the toothless, with butter, tea, and coffee. Fruit and cakes for the children, and, tell it not in Gath, a screw of tobacco for an old man, and a pinch of snuff for his wife. Oliver became pleased and proud of his basket. He always found it made him a pleasant and welcome visitor. All he had to do was within the reach of his present abilities, and happy indeed it would have been for him if all his occupations from his childhood had been measured by the same standard.

His perplexities respecting the future management of his time grew in seriousness as the hour for his brother's reappearance drew near. He consulted Charlotte on the subject, and was assured by her that if he made the most of his time, he would be able to continue his work with the basket, and have some hours to spare during the day for the company of his brother, as well as to prepare his reading lesson for his father in the evening.

'Neither you nor Miss Gordon,' observed Oliver, 'would like me to leave you in your work.'

'Oh, certainly not,' replied Charlotte. 'We should be both, I am sure, sorry to lose you.'

'Then I will tell Jesse so, as soon as I see him, and I daresay, after the first two or three days, he will not want me to be with him much, and then I can always go out with you and Miss Gordon. I am glad I spoke to you, for now I shall know what to do.'

Whatever fears he might still have that Jesse would want to take him from his occupation, they were very soon dissipated on that young gentleman reaching home. So far was he from wanting him to accompany him in his walks, or when out with his gun, that he strongly recommended him to keep on good terms with the ladies, and continue with them in his useful and charitable work.

'That is very kind of you,' said Oliver, 'and I am very much obliged to you for your good advice.'

Jesse was particularly full of business at that time. He had thought over very seriously the conversation he had overheard between the two gentlemen in the hotel at Brighton respecting the late Sir Henry Harewood and his son. He would have taken little heed of what they said, had not the idea presented itself to his mind that the young lady spoken of was the mother of the two orphan children that Lady Harewood so generously protected. It might be only fancy, but if it was so, the more he thought of it the stronger the fancy became.

Since Miss Montag had engrossed so much of his attention, and more especially since he had declared his love to her, he could not help feeling greatly interested in her early life. He knew from a child she had been acquainted with some few German words, of which she could give no account of how or where she had learnt them. All that she could say was that she had known them as long as she could remember anything. These few German words, he believed, had had much to to do in attracting his mother's attention so pointedly to her and her brother, as she had spent some years in Germany before her marriage, and was greatly attached to the language and the people of the country.

'What so likely, then,' he argued with himself, 'that if the account he had listened to at Brighton

was correct, after the death of Mr Henry Harewood, his wife, true or false, as the case might
be, unacknowledged as she was, should have
fallen into a state of poverty, and, as a last
resource, made her way to Woodfield with
the intention of claiming the protection of any
part of the family she might find there.'

He must gather up every incident of their
first appearance in the park, and keep them
fresh in his mind, so that he might be able to
join them together with any new information
he could find, of which he would instantly go
in search.

He knew Mrs Brown, the old nurse, to whose
care he understood the children were, in the first
instance, committed, was always very curious
to learn all that was passing around her, and
that if she had remarked anything in particular
in them when they were brought to her, she
would not be likely to have forgotten it.   Then
he more than half suspected that the unprin-
cipled servant spoken of by the gentlemen was
no other than Lea, his father's old steward.

With respect to that suspicion, strong, however, as it might be, a little thought convinced
him that he must be very careful.   Lea would
be the link to join the past and present together
if he could get sufficient evidence to prove that

the supposed marriage did take place, and that two children, a boy and a girl, resulted from it. But as Lea could not truthfully say a word of what he knew of the matter without condemning himself, it was fairly to be expected that he would not voluntarily utter that one word, much more enter into a narrative that would prove so injurious to his character.

Yes, he must be very cautious in making his attack upon Lea. He must learn all he could from others, and then close suddenly upon him and frighten him into a confession of the whole truth as far as it had come before him. Then there was his father, Sir Edward, all that a stranger could know of the case must at the time of the appearance of the poor lady and her children have been known to him.

But he would not mention the subject that was thus engrossing his thoughts to his father until he had confessed to him his love for Miss Montag. To do so he feared might involve him in a new trouble. Supposing his father disapproved of his declaration to the lady, it might be the means of placing obstacles in the way of the inquiry he was bent upon.

He did not reach home on his return from Brighton till late in the evening, in consequence of his having gone on to London in the hope

of obtaining some information of the movements of the two gentlemen he so much desired
again to meet. But they had passed away as
shadows from the housetop, and had left no
mark that he could find of their existence
behind them.

The first thing to be done on the morning
after his arrival at home, was to take his gun
and go down to the keeper's house to make
himself acquainted with the state of affairs in
and about the woods. Of course he found an
opportunity of speaking to Lizzie, but he could
not venture to tell her what had occurred since
they parted at Brighton, lest he should unnecessarily excite her, and make her restless
and unhappy.

He was therefore obliged to content himself
by saying he had undertaken a little private
business that would perhaps require his whole
attention for a few days, which he must have
out of hand before he could speak to his father
of their engagement. The delay will be but
for a few days at the most, and in the meantime, if a favourable opportunity presents itself,
I shall not fail to avail myself of it. Can you
trust me ?

'I should be unworthy of your love if I
could not,' murmured Lizzie.

They had no time for a lengthened conversation. Mr Smith was within sight and nearly within hearing, while they were together. But what was wanting in thoughtfully expressed words, was more than compensated for by the bright and trusting eyes with which they regarded each other.

Mrs Smith was at her wits' end to discover if they had met at Brighton. By indirect means she had sought to discover from Miss Montag how the matter stood, but in vain. She would have put the question directly to her, had she not continued to hope that she would learn all she wished to know without appearing at all interested in the matter.

She had a shrewd suspicion that they had met, from certain broken sentences that escaped from the lips of little Georgie, in which Jesse's name appeared very prominent. He was too young to give any connected account of what he had seen or heard ; but his mother felt almost assured, from his behaviour, that there were incidents that had occurred at Brighton still floating in his mind which could arise from no other cause than the meeting together of Mr Jesse and Miss Montag.

What they chose to do, she decided after thinking over the affair for some time very seriously, was of course no business of hers. But she was a mother, and almost felt that she stood in that relation to Lizzie, and therefore she could not with a clear conscience see any wrong doing, and remain silent. At length her curiosity grew so strong to learn the real state of affairs, that she resolved she would wait upon accident no longer, but speak openly of her fears to Lizzie ; before, however, she did so, like a sensible woman, she thought it would be as well if she mentioned her intention to her husband.

She would have done so before the death of Philip, had she not feared it would lead to a great commotion. Now that fear no longer existed, but the necessity for something to be done was more pressing than ever.

' I dare say it is all right for you to keep your eyes open in and about your own house,' said Smith, interrupting her in the midst of her story, ' but I can't understand why you should go out of your way to look into every hole and corner in search of other people's business. If Mr Jesse is a little struck with Lizzie's good looks, she is a prudent girl, and no harm, I should think, would come of it. He will soon be going, I am told, away to Oxford, and I dare say he will see plenty of pretty faces there to drive the present nonsense out of his head, if he has got any in it.'

'But you don't consider—'

'Don't consider! What is there to consider?' cried Smith, interrupting her. 'Do you think no one has eyes but yourself? Have you seen anything wrong going on between them? No, of course you have not, nor have I; and more than that, I don't think either of us is likely to.'

'It is to prevent—'

'Prevent dogs and cats. Prevent what?' again broke in Smith. 'Do you want me to think that Miss Montag is a fool, and Mr Jesse a scamp, because if you do, you have rather a tough job before you, I can tell you?'

'Then you think I had better not speak to her?'

'Speak to her as much as you like, but don't go and put your nonsense into her head, and then think you found it there.'

'I can't make you understand.'

'Then don't try,' retorted Smith. 'It will be quite time enough for you to manage other people's business when you have none of your own to attend to.'

Mrs Smith felt herself beaten at all points, and was obliged to give up the contest, though she was far from being satisfied that events would pass off so easily and quietly as her husband seemed to think they would.

'I am glad to see you so active this morning,' said Sir Edward to Jesse, as he met him in the hall, with his gun in his hand, returning from his walk.

'I have been down to see Smith, and have a little talk with him of what he has been doing in my absence, and to learn how his new assistant is coming on.'

'Did you see Dixon?' asked Sir Edward.

'No; but I heard he was at his work again, and doing very well.'

'We must not lose sight of him,' observed Sir Edward. 'I am afraid I was a little too hard upon him.'

'You could not help it, thinking as you did.'

'No, not under the circumstances as they were presented to my mind. But I am heartily glad that the affair is over.'

'And that it ended as it did,' said Jesse; 'had it not been attended by the death of poor Lea.'

As they sat at breakfast Jesse led the conversation to the brother of Miss Montag and his *protégé* — the mischief of the parish.

'I suppose you have done nothing more with that wild boy yet?'

'It is time something was done with him, I

think,' exclaimed Grace, ' or he will soon break his neck, or hang himself, or— Well, I do not know what he will do, he is such a wild boy.'

' What mischief has he done now ?' asked Jesse.

' I don't know that he has done much mischief,' said Grace ; 'but we are told he is fond of getting into all sorts of odd and dangerous places. First he is on the top of the highest tree, then on the roof of a cottage talking to the inmates down the chimney, then he is in the bucket at the well asking his schoolfellows to let him down for a drop of water. Then he has a bonfire from the loose stuff under the trees, and dancing about over it as if fire had no power to hurt him.'

' He is a lively boy,' observed Charlotte, ' but I do not think he is so bad as some people say he is.'

' He is lively enough, that is certain,' said Oliver, ' and dances about round us when I am out with you and Miss Gordon as if he wished to frighten some sweets out of my basket.'

' And does he ever succeed ?' inquired Jesse.

' Yes, almost always. I think Miss Gordon likes him very much, for she comes to me and pokes about in the basket, and I do believe it is to find the best she can for him.'

'You are not jealous, I hope?' said Grace.

'Jealous? oh no!' replied Oliver; 'only I don't see why he should always have the best looked out for him.'

'They say children take after their parents,' observed Jesse. 'I wonder who Mr Montag took after when he chose such a boy as that to be so much attached to.'

'He never had any parents. Did he, papa?' asked Grace.

'You mean,' said Jesse, 'that it is not known who his parents were?'

'Yes, that is what I mean,' said Grace, her face growing very red at the idea of the ridiculous mistake she had made.

'Poor fellow!' said Sir Edward, 'I am afraid both he and his sister will, to the end of their days, remain in ignorance of their parentage.'

'I could never understand,' observed Jesse, 'why it was so difficult to discover from whence they came.'

'Take the problem yourself, Jesse, and see what you can make of it. A cold autumnal night, a poor starving woman, speechless when first seen, two crying children by her side, infants I may say, shivering with cold, all thinly clad, and on whose clothes, on the strictest search being made, no distinct mark of any kind could be found. Yes, take the notes, Jesse, to your room, and see what you, with the aid of all your books, can make of them.'

'I think,' said Jesse, 'I would not appeal to my dead books, but rather to all the living evidence that could be procured.'

'And where would you find any?' asked his father.

'I think I have heard,' replied Jesse, 'that you have no doubt their parents were Germans.'

'That idea was the only clue we could get to work upon,' said Sir Edward, 'and that rested on no better foundation than from the few sounds the children uttered, which your mother said were German words that she had heard at Munich.'

'And were their clothes of German texture?'

'No; I was told they were all English.'

'Respecting the German words, I suppose there can be no doubt?'

'Your mother said there was not, and she was well skilled in the German tongue and its varieties of expression in different parts of the empire. She repeated certain sounds to the children, which they readily caught and made their own; but I am far from certain that their German was not more of your mother's teaching than from any previous knowledge they had of it.'

'They have both much to be grateful for,' said Jesse.

'To your mother,' rejoined Sir Edward; 'yes, much.' Then after a pause he added, 'I may say everything, for she it was who caused them to be lifted up from their miserable state to that which they now occupy.'

'And was everything done that could be done,' asked Jesse, 'to settle the question of their birth?'

'We thought so at the time,' replied Sir Edward, 'and I have since had no reason to doubt the justness of the conclusion we then came to. We advertised the case in the papers, and we sent Lea into Germany to make inquiries. He had travelled a good deal in the country, and freely offered himself for the service. But it was all to no purpose, neither from the advertisements nor his inquiries did we obtain the slightest information.'

'Lea,' said Jesse; 'do you mean the poor fellow we have just lost?'

'No, but his father, who left the room a minute since. You have heard that he was the late Sir Henry's servant, and travelled with him.'

'I should like to hear his account of the manner in which he conducted his search,' said Jesse.

'I do not see what pleasure or profit you could derive from it,' rejoined Sir Edward. Some events are better forgotten than remembered, and this appears to be one of them, as nothing can now result from a renewal of the inquiry but vexation and disappointment.'

'You know, papa,' said Jesse, 'I am fond of adventures, and Lea, I should think, must have met with many in his passing from place to place in his search. I should like to have a talk with him about it.'

'If you will keep your conversation to yourselves,' replied Sir Edward, 'you may have a whole day to talk it over; but to return to Edmund Montag's *protégé*. I think he will have to be sent away to a school at a distance.'

'I have a little writing to do this morning,' said Jesse, 'and I have promised to meet Smith at eleven o'clock; but I shall avail myself of your permission to have a long talk with Lea very shortly.'

CHAPTER VIII.

WITHIN a month from the day when Mr Cresswell sent his determination respecting his son-in-law to his friend at Marseilles, two Englishmen were seated together in a private room at an hotel in that city. By the manner in which they were dressed, it was evident they wished to be considered as gentlemen to whom a few pounds more or less was of little consequence.

The younger of the two was a man of about forty, whose jaunty air, coupled with features upon which dissipation had set its mark, showed unmistakably to what class of society he belonged. The other was a little, white-haired, old man primly attired in a suit of dark clothes carefully fitted to his slender body.

They had just met after a brief separation. Their behaviour to each other on the present occasion, whatever it might have been at some former time, was not indicative of perfect equality, though there was a freedom about it which showed that their acquaintance was not of yesterday.

'We cannot always control our luck,' said Circum, the elder of the two; 'but it is very awkward to find a gentleman without a pound when one wants it so badly.'

'That is often your case, my good friend,' said Claypole Lyson, for he it was who sat in the opposite chair.

'But not the less unpleasant on that account.'

'Well,' said Lyson, 'I am sorry for you, but I cannot help you. I am as hard-up as yourself; and you must know that you are not the only unlucky fellow in the world. The fates have been against me for the last month. Cards and dice have been equally against me. By no possible trick within my reach have I been able to put a single pound in my purse.'

'Ah!' said Circum, 'but you can afford to be independent of luck; you have rich relations that in hard times you can fall back upon, and so are not obliged to live upon the ups and downs of life as I am.'

'Rich relations,' said Lyson, 'and so they are

likely to be for the trifle I can get out of them.'

' You get your quarterly supplies ? '

' I have had them up to the present time,' said Lyson ; ' but because I have asked for a pound or two extra, I am told that I must be quiet or I shall have no more.'

' But you are not disposed to be quiet for an idle threat like that ?   It is very hard, I know, to bleed some people, but there are few, I imagine, who can perform the operation more scientifically than you.'

' Tools become blunt with using.'

' Not in your hands.'

' Listen,' said Lyson, ' and you shall judge. I lately came across here in Marseilles an old friend of my dear old father-in-law, and being as a matter of course a little short of the needful at the time, I entreated him to let me have a trifle on the old gentleman's account, to join a party bound for the Holy Land, or some other out-of-the-way place.   I was obliged to put it on pretty strong, and to submit to all sorts of questioning before I could get the half of what I wanted ; and now, as I am trying for the other half, I am told to be very careful, or my quarterly remittance will be stopped ; and the most provoking part of the business is, I have good reason for believing, by a telegram that was sent from this place, that an old enemy of mine, Sir Edward Harewood, is in the plot against me.'

' Harewood!' said Circum ; 'he cannot be a son of the late Sir Henry ? '

' No ; he is his nephew.'

' Ah !' I remember the particulars of the case now ; the old man lost his son and died childless.'

'That is saying more than circumstances will warrant,' said Lyson.

' I mean legitimate,' said Circum.

' Ah ! that's another matter.'

' But,' replied Circum, 'it is sometimes not a very difficult matter to manufacture a little legitimacy. If it would answer your purpose, I think I could assist you to make this Sir Edward shake in his shoes.'

' You don't say so !' exclaimed Lyson.

' True,' replied Circum. 'Years ago I did the late Sir Henry's son a little service, that so nearly supplied him with a wife that it will take a fortune at this time of day to prove she was not a real one.'

' But how would that affect the present man ? ' asked Lyson.

'Suppose,' said Circum, 'the wife I helped

the youth to had children, and one of them a son, who would set up a claim to the entailed estate, what would you say to that?'

'Why,' said Lyson, 'the bare possibility of the thing warms my heart to think of it. But where is the son?'

'That we have to discover,' replied Circum, 'which I think would not be a very difficult matter, supposing we could raise the needful to cover a little travelling expenses to look for him.'

'And so your fine scheme rests upon no better foundation than that,' said Lyson sarcastically. 'Throw away money to look for a child that perchance never existed.'

'Not so,' said Circum. 'Whether the boy exists now I do not know, but that he did exist I am well assured, as I know that, within a year of the marriage, the young wife presented the world with twins—a boy and a girl.'

'Are you sure of that?' asked Lyson.

'As sure as I am now sitting before you,' was the reply. 'I was a little short of money at the time, and endeavoured to raise the wind by a visit to the young gentleman at the village where I had witnessed his marriage.'

'Well, and what then?' said Lyson.

'The gentleman was not to be found,' replied

Circum ; 'and the silly girl with her twins appealed to me for help, which brought my profitable interest in the affair to an end, and caused me to lose sight of the young family. But with a little trouble and expense I could renew my acquaintance, and lend you a helping hand on, if not to fortune, at least to revenge.'

'And all on the chance,' said Lyson, 'after nearly twenty years, of finding the twins alive ?'

'Only one of them,' argued Circum. 'Whether the girl is alive or dead is of little consequence.'

'It does not appear a very promising case,' said Lyson ; 'and I am as poor as a church mouse. My remittance will be due in the course of a week, but it is already nearly all booked. Will you want much for your search ?'

'Not more than ten pounds at present. I have an old friend now in Paris, who has friends living near the village where the marriage took place. With his aid I can inexpensively make a searching inquiry.'

'There is no doubt in this ?' said Lyson suspiciously.

'No ; honour to the backbone.'

'You shall have the ten pounds; but woe to you if you only attempt to deceive me.'

'Fear nothing. Did you say in a week?'

'Yes; and immediately afterwards I will write to my dear old father-in-law for a trifle more. I have not written to him for some time now, and only heard of him through his friend here, who may not have acted quite fairly between us. If I can only strike him on the right key, he may send me the means of sailing off briskly on our new course. If he proves disagreeable, and orders his banker to stop the supply, I must go over to Downend, and have a word or two with him about this Sir Edward, who, I suspect, with his conniv- ance, has been taking my place beside my wife, as I know he once wished to do.'

'Better and better,' cried Circum; 'we will attack him on two sides at once, and if we can do nothing more, we can bleed him pretty freely to keep us quiet.'

'I think,' said Lyson thoughtfully, 'I must get you to go over first and see what they are about. I can give you an introduction to my father, with whom you can stop for a few days. You will find my two amiable sisters there, who think me little less than an angel. I will write to them, and then, you may depend, they will

receive you with open arms. But talking of
angels reminds me that I have an engagement
to meet one at the cathedral door a few minutes
from this time. Write to your friend in Paris,
and we will talk over the affair again to-
morrow.'

While this diabolical plot was being hatched
in Marseilles, Jesse, bent on the object he had
in view of discovering the parentage of Miss
Montag and her brother, called at the cottage
in the green lane, where he found Mrs Brown
in great trouble about her old friend Mrs Dicks,
whom we have known as Jasper's old crony.

'Quite well yesterday,' she said, 'and with
her daughter Nancy busy about her work, and
to-day stretched out stiff and cold, ready for her
coffin.'

'Poor old body!' said Jesse; 'I did not
hear of her death.'

'She's gone,' said Mrs Brown; 'and although
she was a little touchy at times, she has left
many a worse woman behind her.'

'How will their business go on now?' said
Jesse. 'Will Nancy be able to manage it
alone?'

'She has just told me,' replied Mrs Brown,
'that she doesn't mean to go on alone, for she
means to marry Jasper Gotley.'

'Jasper Gotley!' echoed Jesse. 'What!— my brother's servant? Why, she must be forty years old, and he is not more than eighteen!'

'I told her, sir, that people would be talking about it; but she said that was her business, and she didn't care a straw what people said— that she meant to marry Jasper, and would have done so before, only her mother wouldn't let her speak to him about it.'

'But what does Jasper say to it?' asked Jesse.

'I don't know, sir. He has a word for everybody, and it is not easy to know what he means. She said he was getting too old for Mr Oliver, and that he should get a better place. He is not likely to be won by her beauty, but there is a good business, and I believe her mother has left her some money, and that may prove a little tempting to him.'

Here their talk was broken in upon by Stephen Elvin, who rushed in from school, ready to take down his dinner, as he said, 'in no time,' that he might go out to play.

'Dinner is not quite ready yet,' said Mrs Brown. 'Come in again presently.'

'All right,' said the boy; 'go and make myself more hungry;' and off he bounded from the door as suddenly as he had approached it.

'He seems pretty full of life,' remarked Jesse.

'Full of life, sir!' repeated Mrs Brown. 'I think he is life itself.'

'And not over careful of it,' added Jesse.

'No; that he is not,' replied Mrs Brown. 'If he were, I should never have had him here with me; that plunge into the river saved him from the union.'

'And at the same time saved the life of Edmund Montag,' said Jesse.

'Yes, and I can never think of it without trembling.'

'I heard an account of it when I was at school; but I believe I never had the full particulars,' said Jesse.

'It did not take five minutes about, sir,' replied Mrs Brown. 'It happened one evening after school, when Edmund and I were out for a walk. As we were strolling along by the side of the river, he stooped and leaned over the edge of the bank to pick some flowers that were growing near the water. I don't know how it was, and I don't think I ever shall know. Whether the bank gave way under his feet, or he became giddy, I can't say, but all at once I saw him stagger for a moment, and then fall forward into the river. The current was strong and the water deep, and although Edmund could swim a little, he was carried away from the bank, and would have been drowned, I believe, had not the boy who has just left us suddenly slipped down from a tree and plunged into the river to his assistance.

'We learnt afterwards that he had climbed up the tree to make a swing from one of the branches. He had the cord in his hand, and leaving one end of it with me he floated like a cork in the water with the other end to Edmund, and called out to me, "Pull away, Mrs Brown, and we will soon be back again."

'How I pulled I don't know; but as I said, in five minutes it was all over, and they were both dripping wet on the bank again.

'Edmund thanked the boy very heartily, and the more so as during the afternoon he had felt obliged to report him to the headmaster for having played off one of his mischievous tricks upon a schoolfellow.

'As soon as we reached the house, and Edmund had changed his dress, he said he could not rest until he had been to see if the boy had gone home, and been properly cared for. His mother was a poor widow in a very delicate state of health, and did not live many years afterwards. On her death-bed I, by desire of

Edmund, told her that he would take charge of her boy when she was gone. The poor soul died while blessing him for his goodness.'

'And then Edmund gave him in charge to you?'

'Yes,' replied Mrs Brown, 'and a blessing has seemed to rest upon him ever since. He is now, you know, sir, the second master in a good school, and in a fair way, I hope, of rising to a higher position.'

'You are greatly attached to him?'

'I have reason to be, sir,' said Mrs Brown, as she wiped the tears from her eyes, 'for he has been very good to me.'

'You had him in training many years?'

'Yes; he came to me a baby child, and left me but a few months since a full grown man.'

'He has much to be grateful for on account of the care you took of him during his infancy. Did he not sometimes wish to learn who his parents were?'

'A few years since he appeared very anxious to know all he could about them.'

'But you could not give him a satisfactory answer?'

'No, I could only tell him what every one near the Hall knew.'

'It seems very strange,' said Jesse, 'that no marks could be found on their clothes to lead to their identification?'

'Ah! poor things,' said Mrs Brown, 'they had nothing on them worthy the name of clothes. They were mere rags hanging about them, and they did not appear to have ever been made for them. I told Mr Lea, who came from Lady Harewood to see them, that I thought perhaps the poor woman in her distress had sold their good clothes and bought the old rags just to cover them, for she could scarcely hope they would keep them warm.'

'And what did Lea say?' asked Jesse.

'Called me an old simpleton for imagining such a thing.'

'But had he formed any opinion of the matter himself?' asked Jesse.

'He said he supposed they were only common tramps, and it was a pity there was so much fuss made about them. I told him they had not the skins of tramps, when he became very angry, and told me that it was a pity that I had not to go away into Germany to find out who they were instead of him, as he supposed I thought I could do the work better than he could.'

'When do you expect to see Edmund again?'

'I don't know, sir; but I am sure he will come as soon as he can.'

'I should like to speak to him about your little fellow Stephen, who, I see, is coming back for his dinner.'

With a hop, skip, and a jump the boy came up the garden walk, and, meeting the visitor at the door, gave him a military salute and passed into the cottage.

What Jesse had just heard tended to confirm the opinion he had lately formed of Lea. Strolling away from the door of Mrs Brown, he made for the most retired part of the park. He wished to be alone. He did not even require the presence of his beloved Lizzie, so earnest was he without loss of time to settle in his own mind how he should attack the person of him who, he believed, had the secret he wished to discover hidden away in his memory. 'If it were his son,' he thought, 'and he were still alive, I should have but little trouble with him; but the elder is such a curious old stick, that I don't quite know how best to handle him.'

I thought, when I began my inquiry this morning, that if I could learn as much as I now know, I would boldly charge Lea with his duplicity in keeping as a secret from my father the knowledge I am certain he must possess; but

he seems very shaky, and if I attack him too
suddenly I may throw him into a fit or something of the kind, when he would be unable to
tell me what, however unwillingly, I may get
from him by a gentler mode of treatment.   I
wish I could speak to some one on the subject,
but I cannot, and therefore I must be content to
work it out alone.

'If Lea knew the poor woman who died in the
park, he deserves—well, I will not say what;
but if he knew the mother, he must know the
true history of the children.   Oh dear! I think
I cannot stretch out my patience much longer.
If he cannot satisfy me in every particular, he
can tell me much that will help me bravely on
in my investigations.

'Perhaps if I were to call and see Mr Gordon,
he might be able to assist me.   Doubtless he
buried the poor wanderer, and was interested
in her fate.   I may not get much from him;
but a little bit here and a little bit there, when
put together, may lead to some important result.   One thing I can learn from him, that is
certain.   If there was anything strange in the
conduct of Lea at the time he must have remarked it.'

A few yards from the vicarage Jesse met Mr
Gordon, and, after having been complimented

on the benefit he had received from his visit to Brighton, entered immediately on the object of his visit by alluding to the lively little fellow he had just parted from at the cottage in the lane.

As they entered the vicarage, Mr Gordon said,—

'I am told by some people who profess to be skilled in the management of boys, that if Stephen Elvin is left much longer with Mrs Brown he will become the pest of the village.'

'I think my father intends to consult Mr Montag on the propriety of sending him away to a school at a distance.'

'Yes,' replied Mr Gordon ; 'he mentioned the subject to me, and I was glad to hear he proposed to consult Mr Montag.'

'It is very curious,' remarked Jesse, 'to observe how far-reaching an act of kindness is. Had my mother not made provision for Mr Montag and his sister, the little fellow would now most likely have been a pauper in the union.'

'Yes,' said Mr Gordon ; 'and we cannot be too thankful that it is so.'

'My mother's care seems to have been well bestowed.'

'I know no young man at the present time,' replied Mr Gordon, 'who is likely to make a better use of his advantages than Mr Montag.'

'It is very sad we can form no idea of his family.'

'Very,' said Mr Gordon; 'it has been a hopeless case since his first appearance here. Your good mother was very anxious about it, and I believe spent much time and money on the inquiry.'

'Did she employ trustworthy agents?'

'There can be no doubt of that,' replied Mr Gordon, 'as the chief one was your father's old servant.   Poor old fellow, he was hardly fit for the duty at his time of life; and I think he has to this day scarcely recovered from the anxiety and labour it occasioned him.'

'Have you ever conversed with him upon the subject?'

'Yes—many times,' rejoined Mr Gordon; 'though not of late.   He has pointed out to me the trials he had to contend against, as he daily met with disappointment that at times quite disabled him.   Still I must confess—'

At this point the conversation was interrupted by the entrance of a maid-servant with a very red face, and in a state of considerable excitement.

' Please, sir,' she said, ' here is Nancy Dicks wants to see you.'

' Did you ask her business?' inquired Mr Gordon.

' Yes, sir ; but she said her business was no business of mine, and she would not tell me what it was.'

' Say I am engaged, and will see her another time.'

' I told her you were engaged, sir,' replied the indignant maid ; ' but she said she didn't care for that. She wanted to see you, and she must see you, and she would see you.'

' To be taken by storm,' said Mr Gordon to Jesse. ' Poor soul! I suppose you know she has just lost her mother. They were a curious pair, but I believe they were in their way attached to each other.'

' I don't think they were at all, sir,' interposed the maid.

' Very well,' said Mr Gordon ; ' tell her again I am engaged, but if she wants to see me very much she may come in.'

' Master's too easy,' thought the maid, ' and that makes the people so impudent when they come to the house.' Nevertheless she obeyed, and silently left the room. In a few seconds she re-appeared, and, throwing the door wide

open, left the way clear for the entrance of
Nancy Dicks.

Had the gentlemen not been well acquainted
with her general appearance, they would have
doubtless looked with surprise upon the comical
figure before them.   Nancy, though forty years
of age, was not more than four feet ten inches
in height ; but though nature had cut her short
in stature, she had been very liberal to her in
bone and muscle.   She was not, as some people
said, as thick as she was long, but with half an
eye one might see she was of a good solid
shape and substance.

A round, red, fat face, with little twinkling
grey eyes, made her countenance not very pre-
possessing, though it was generally covered
with an insinuating smile, or what was vulgarly
called a broad grin.   On her head she wore a
large overlapping bonnet, much more common
fifty years since than in the present day.   Of
her underclothing one could see nothing, as
from her neck to her feet she was shut up in a
man's great rough coat, with a high collar and a
flowing cape.   Her boots gave notice of her
approach, being of the hobnail kind.

A short black-thorn stick, with a bit of cord
attached to it, being an apology for a whip,
ornamented her left hand, while with her right

she appeared to be fumbling in her pocket for some hidden treasure.

'Sorry to trouble, sir,' said Nancy, as she cleared the doorway, her face covered with her most winning smile, 'but as mother is gone, and I am left all alone, I mean to get married.'

'Yes,' said Mr Gordon, returning her smile.

'And I want you to marry me.'

'Me,' said Mr Gordon, a little startled at the request, hastily concluding that Nancy's late trouble had damaged her wits.

'I mean,' said Nancy, seeing that Mr Gordon did not immediately follow up his me with any other words, 'I mean, you see, sir, I want you to tie me and Jasper together.'

'Tie you together!' said Mr Gordon, purposely appearing not to understand her.

'Yes, marry us.'

'Oh, you wish to marry Jasper?'

'Yes,' replied Nancy, 'that's just what I do wish, and what I mean to do. Mother's left me all her money—three hundred pounds—and I mean to have a husband, but my sisters, who haven't got nothing, say I sha'n't, but I will for all them.'

'But your mother is not buried?'

'Oh, we will bury her first; I only come

now to put the banns up, that my sisters may see what I mean to do.'

'If that is all you had to tell me,' said Mr Gordon, 'you need not have come to me. Had you given your notice to the clerk, it would have been sufficient.'

'I did tell him,' said Nancy, 'but he only laughed, and said he'd see to it. So I made him write it down in his book, and I paid him beforehand, that he might be quite sure I meant what I said. And now, sir,' she continued, in her most coaxing manner, 'if you will please tell me what I shall have to pay you I will settle that too, because you see, sir, I don't want to have any mistake, and let my sisters say, I told you the parson wouldn't do it.'

'Keep your money,' said Mr Gordon, 'I will remember you offered it to me. But tell me, why did not Jasper do this for you?'

'Oh, he's a little shy-like, sir, and so I thought I had better do it myself, as he might make a blunder about it, because you see he has not thought of it as I have.'

'You have been thinking of it for some time, then?'

'Oh yes, ever so long, sir, only mother would not let me talk about it.'

' And you are quite resolved now.'

' Oh yes, sir, next Sunday week, please, for the first time. I shall come to church on purpose to see it's all right, and so I thank you, and bid you good day, for Jasper is waiting for me outside.'

' Good morning !' returned Mr Gordon.

As soon as she was gone, Jesse threw down the paper he had held before his face to prevent his laughing from being seen, and said,—

' If Jasper is taken captive by such a figure, I shall be surprised.'

' But the three hundred pounds !'

' The rascal, would he marry her for that ?'

' It would not be a very singular case if he did,' rejoined Mr Gordon.

' And will you really marry them ?'

' I do not see how I can avoid doing so, if they attend to the direction laid down for their guidance in the Prayer Book, and from Nancy's manner I should think she has been studying it. But I must make some inquiry about them, and if I find reason to think their union would prove an unhappy one, endeavour to prevent them from proceeding any further in the matter. Nancy may have a soft head, but she has given us proof that she has a strong will, and it is very possible no one will be able to turn her from her purpose.'

'You were saying something when she entered,' observed Jesse, in connection with Lea's investigation of the case of the poor woman and her children.'

'Yes,' replied Mr Gordon, 'that there were some points in the old man's statement which I could not understand, but as you appear interested in his proceedings, I will, if you like, take an opportunity of meeting him with you in one of his little walks, and hear him go over his tale once more.'

'His account of his journey,' said Jesse, 'will doubtless prove very entertaining to me, as I do not remember to have ever heard him speak one word on the subject. I hope it will not bore you to hear the old story over again?'

'It will not do that,' said Mr Gordon; 'but we may have to wait a day or two for a favourable interview, as you do not wish to make a very formal affair of it.'

'Oh no, certainly not,' said Jesse.

CHAPTER IX.

N O sooner had Lyson secured his quarterly stipend than he turned to the consideration of the letter he had resolved to send to his father, preparatory to another he purposed writing to Mr Cresswell. It was some time since he had last addressed his father, and when he sat down to commence his task, he discovered that it was likely to give him a considerable amount of trouble.

If his object had been merely to write a friendly letter to his father or his sisters, the case would have been very different. He knew that anything he might say to them would be scanned by friendly eyes. That if the sentences he used would bear two meanings, they would fix upon the most favourable one, and that any excuse he might offer for past neglect in his correspondence, or of the cause

of his present want of money, would be received by his sisters, at least, without question
as a veritable truth.

But on the present occasion his letter must
be written in a tone and manner that critical
and unfriendly eyes might look upon without
suspicion of the real object he had in view—
that object being to get Mr Cresswell's purse
more readily opened to his hand. By way of
introduction, he might beg his father or sister
to send him a remittance, though that could be
only as a matter of form, as he well knew he
had already drained them to the last pound.

The letter would doubtless be shown to Mr
Cresswell, and hence the necessity of great
carefulness being bestowed upon its composi-
tion ; and he was even doubtful if its exhibition
would end there—whether it would not fall
under the eye of Sir Edward Harewood, of
whom he had at the same time the most in-
tense fear and bitter hatred. Let a man injure
you, and he will hate you for ever, says the
proverb, and this Lyson was unconsciously
proving as he meditated on the kind of letter
he would write.

' It is bad enough,' he thought, ' to be over-
hauled by the old man, but to be picked to
pieces by that pompous fellow, Harewood, is

more than I can stand. Yet the letter must be written, that I may have the means of carrying out my venture of clipping his well-plumed wings. Let me but get hold of a descendant of the late Sir Henry, and, legitimate or illegitimate, I will lead him a dance that, before I have done with him, he shall be as poor as I am. If he chooses to go out of his way to fight against me, I will take him on his own terms and repay him with interest. If I fail in that, I will attack him through my wife. My sisters have let me in a little to the notion of the kind of relationship that exists between them, and then I have his letters, in which he treats of his love for his dear Edith. Certainly it was before I married her. But what of that? Can I not show that she was no sooner my wife than I made an unpleasant discovery, and that he induced her to leave my house and return to England to live near him, that he might the more easily carry on his illicit intercourse with her? That, I think, will make about as pretty a case to be brought into court as one might expect to meet with in the course of a century. Armed with my two guns, if I do not bring down my prey, I have studied men and women to little purpose, and may as well go back again to my cradle. Two or three thousand a-

year is the least they can offer me, and the
least I will take, to keep me from plunging
one into poverty, and covering the name of the
other with shame and infamy.   But this is all
beside the question in hand.   My present
business is to write a letter to my father, which
may induce him to go to Mr Cresswell and get
me the means of commencing war against my
old rival.   He has heaps of gold, which he has
not the heart to spend himself, or give me the
chance of doing, further than by my little quarterly driblets, for which I am to hold myself as
a banished man from wife and country.   Now,
then, for a start !'

Having written a few lines, he stopped, and
muttered,—

' No ; that will not do ; I must try again.'

After repeating this three or four times, and
angrily tearing up and destroying the paper, he
at last succeeded in some measure in accom-
plishing his purpose.

The letter was finished, stamped, and ready
for the post ; still he was not satisfied with his
performance.   He turned it over in his hand,
and appeared on the point of tearing it open.
He did not, however, do so ; but muttering,
' It must go,' put on his hat, and walked out to
the office.

Great was the commotion the letter occasioned on its reaching its destination at the vicarage of Downend. The vicar was by this time barely the shadow of his former self. Rheumatic pains flying about his body, with an occasional touch of the gout in his feet and hands, had reduced him to a very unwholesome and shaky condition. Nor can his mental faculties be brought more favourably under notice. His chief occupation appeared now to consist in mourning over the past, complaining of the present, and dreading the future. He was altogether in a pitiable plight; whether deservedly so or not, we will not venture to determine.

There was a time when he could take his bottle of port after dinner, and talk of the ease with which he could perform his duties; but now the control of his house and the parish rested chiefly upon his daughters, while the offices of the church were too often left almost entirely in the inexperienced hands of a young curate. Still he seemed to imagine that the whole burden rested upon his own shoulders; and hence all that came before him met with words expressive of his dissatisfaction, if every occurrence had not been dealt with in accordance to his fancy.

From this it will be seen how unable he was to cope with his heartless and designing son, and to judge how little benefit was likely to result from an application to Mr Cresswell for money.

With trembling hands he opened the letter, and struggled on through a few lines to make himself acquainted with its general contents ; then, wearied with the exertion, he gave it to his eldest daughter, saying,—

'There is nothing new in it that I can see ; all the same as ever—money, money, money !'

'Shall I read it out, papa ?' said Miss Lyson.

'Yes, yes,' murmured her father ; 'but it is of no use. He is not coming home ; he only wants money, [and I have none to send him. It is all gone—his and mine and yours.'

'I think,' said Miss Lyson, after running her 'eye over the letter, 'he does not expect you to send him any ; he only wants you to speak to Mr Cresswell to render him a little extra assistance. Poor fellow ! You know he is always very unfortunate with his money ; and we are unfortunate, too, that we are not able to assist him.'

Then, without further preface, she read the letter through.

'I do not think,' said Dorothy, the younger sister, 'that he is at all unreasonable in what he says. He merely asks you to do him a little service in speaking to Mr Cresswell. You know as well as we do that that gentleman is very rich, to whom the difference of a thousand pounds is not of more consequence than a pound to us.'

'Say ten thousand pounds,' interposed Miss Lyson, 'and I believe you will be much nearer the truth.'

'Yes; I agree with you,' said Dorothy; 'and all that he requires papa to do is to go and beg Mr Cresswell to let him have only a few paltry pounds.'

'And how can I do that?' argued her father. 'You know I can hardly walk across to the church, and I have no carriage now. I do wish my boy had never gone away.'

'But you were willing that he should go?' said Miss Lyson.

'I never thought he would stop away so long,' whined the father.

'As you are not able to go,' said Miss Lyson, 'shall we send to Mr Cresswell and beg him to come to you?'

'I don't know,' said the vicar peevishly; 'I don't want to be troubled. I am not equal to

it. Cannot you go to Mr Cresswell yourself?
You know all about it as well as I do.'

'Oh, papa, how could I go upon such an
errand!'

'And how could I ask him to come here?'
sighed the father.

'You do not like to go alone,' said Dorothy;
'but how would it be if I were to offer to go
with you?'

'Yes, yes, go both of you,' said the vicar,
'and take the letter with you. Perhaps Mr
Cresswell will listen favourably to you, but I
know he would not to me if I were to send to
him to come here.'

'Then we will go,' said Miss Lyson, 'for it
must never be said that we saw our poor
brother in need, and did not go a step out of
our way to help him. Shall we give Mr Cresswell any message from you?'

'You may say to him that if he can oblige
you, I shall be very glad.'

'I hope we shall not find Edith with her
father,' said Miss Lyson to her sister, just as
they were setting out on their charitable errand.

'Oh, I dare say she is out,' replied Dorothy.
'She is to be seen, you know, on the road to
Woodfield almost every day.'

'Yes, and more's the pity,' said Miss Lyson,

'and I only hope she will not quite forget she is a married woman.'

'And so do I,' rejoined Dorothy; 'but it looks very strange, I think, to see her on that road so often where she must expect to meet Sir Edward Harewood, and he a single man. I do not like it at all, and I do not think our dear brother would if he knew it. I just gave him a little hint of how things were going on in my last letter, and I shall do so again when I write.'

'We must not allude to anything of the kind to-day,' observed Miss Lyson, 'though I must say I should like to make Edith understand that I think she is very cruel, if nothing worse, in not sending some of her superfluous cash to her own husband, who has been so much imposed upon.'

With this good-natured, fair-dealing spirit the two sisters approached Elston Court, where, to their great mortification, on their introduction to Mr Cresswell, they found not only his wife and daughter present, but Sir Edward Harewood and his son Oliver.

The usual greetings over, Miss Lyson said rather timidly to Mr Cresswell,—

'Papa gave us a message for you. He would have called himself, but he is too weak and poorly to leave the house to-day.'

'Something about church matters?' said Mr Cresswell inquiringly.

'No, not exactly,' replied Miss Lyson, and then, after a pause, she added, 'he said he hoped I should meet you alone.'

'We have, as you see, none but friends here,' said Mr Cresswell.

'My father,' rejoined Miss Lyson, 'is very nervous and a little exacting to-day, and if I tell him I did not press upon you to see me alone, I am afraid he will be very angry. Do you not think so?' she said, addressing her sister.

'Oh yes, I am certain he would be very angry,' replied Dorothy.

'Then, to prevent discord,' said Mr Cresswell good-naturedly, 'if our friends will excuse us, and you will go with me to the library, we will comply with your father's request.'

'May I come too?' asked Dorothy.

'As you please,' replied Mr Cresswell in his former tone.

They were absent but a very few minutes, and when they returned there was a look of dissatisfaction on the faces of each of the ladies, while on Mr Cresswell's were traces of excitement, which he vainly strove to hide from his wife and Edith.

' As papa will be expecting us back,' said Miss Lyson, in a thick, unsteady voice, ' I am afraid we must not lengthen out our unexpected visit.'

With that the bell was rung, and the two sisters again left the room.

' Rather a formal finish,' said Edith. ' What have you done to them, papa ? '

Mr Cresswell looked at Oliver, who sat near in a listening attitude.

Sir Edward, who was not slow to catch his meaning, immediately said to Oliver,—

' I wish you would go out and see how the weather is likely to be for the next hour or two. If you go to the top of the hill yonder, you will have a good view over a large expanse of country.'

As soon as Oliver was gone, Mr Cresswell, addressing his wife, said,—

' I did not speak before Oliver, for a reason you will understand when I tell you that the business upon which I left you' was concerning a letter the vicar has received from Marseilles. Of which letter I would not say another word if I did not feel assured my silence would give you more uneasiness than anything I have to tell you. I know, although I have not spoken of it, how anxiously during the last few days you have been watching the letter-bag. My blunder has opened your eyes to what is passing, and I cannot close them again.'

'Is the letter from the vicar's son?' asked Sir Edward.

'Yes,' was the reply, 'and, as you may expect, upon the old theme. He is in difficulties again, and has written to his father for money, and on his not being able to supply him with it, requested him to come to me with his letter.'

'And you answered without hesitation, I trust,' said Sir Edward.

'Yes, I begged the ladies to tell their father that I could hold no communication with his son through him. That he had been informed that if he had anything he wished to say to me not to use a third person for the purpose. So you must understand,' he said, addressing his wife and daughter, 'that nothing new has occurred to make you look so alarmed and anxious.'

'It makes me very wretched,' said Edith, 'to know you are so worried on my account.'

'And your mother, too,' said Mr Cresswell playfully, 'to see that you worry yourself so much about me.'

'I wish I could take the whole affair off

your hands,' said Sir Edward ; 'but that is impossible.'

'Many thanks for your kind wish,' rejoined Mr Cresswell. 'It is right that we should help to bear one another's burdens, and as I have sent rather a harsh message to our poor suffering vicar, I think I will take a walk and see him, that he may know I did not wish to distress him.'

'And Oliver and I,' said Sir Edward, 'will, at the same time, set out for home. When may we expect to see you at Woodfield ?'

'Oh, very soon,' replied Mr Cresswell in a rather absent manner.

'Then let it be to-morrow for luncheon.'

'Will you be able to go ?' said Mr Cresswell to his wife.

'Yes, if it is to accompany you,' was the reply.

'Then I think you may expect us,' said Mr Cresswell ; 'but you must not make your luncheon a dinner, or we shall be in trouble with our people when we return, because we have left our appetites behind.'

'That is Mr Cresswell's nonsense,' said his wife ; 'he wishes us to think he is in excellent spirits.'

'Oh yes, I know him of old,' said Sir Edward ;

and so they parted with smiles on their lips, in the vain endeavour to persuade one another that they were all very happy.

For some days after Jesse's conversation with Mr Gordon his patience was sorely tried. The old steward fell ill with an attack of gout, and was confined to his room. His temper, as we have seen, was not naturally of the most amiable character, and this attack rendered him more than ever difficult to deal with. He seemed thoroughly impressed with the idea that every one in the village and Hall was pleased to know that he was out of the way, and loud were his complaints of how the under servants would be going on wasting and spoiling no one knew how much, now that he was not able to get about to look after them.

Sir Edward turned a deaf ear to him. He had full confidence in Mrs Gibson, and he learnt from her that the gout and his temper had more to do with his complaints of the servants than any misconduct on their part. Jesse and Oliver occasionally paid a visit to the sufferer ; the former, it must be confessed, from a slightly interested motive, while Oliver did it out of pure good nature and pity. Jesse endeavoured to turn his visits to account by the many allusions he made to the incidents Lea must have met with in his foreign travels. But the gout held, or seemed to hold, the mastery over his thoughts, and rendered all Jesse's attempts to extract information from him useless.

Oliver was more fortunate with the patient. In his simple way he strove to be amusing without being at all curious about past events. His conversation had special reference to incidents of the day in which one or more of the servants was generally concerned.

'Your deputy, Taylor, seems a trustworthy fellow,' said Oliver.

'Does he?' retorted the old steward. 'I am very glad to hear it, and I only hope he is what he seems to be.'

'Your poor son had a good opinion of him, I think.'

'My son?' rejoined the old man. 'Don't talk to me of him. He was always ready to be fooled by any one, and that made it so much the worse for me.'

'Worse for you!' repeated Oliver.

'Yes; don't you see he made everything I said or did rough and hard. But well, well; perhaps it is all right that it was so. I should have missed him more if he had been like me. Oh dear! where can that whipper-snapper of a doctor be; I wanted him an hour ago.   But instead of his coming here to give me something to take away this horrible pain, I daresay he is, with a long face, hanging over the couch of some young lady, who has pricked her finger and fainted from the loss of a quarter of a drop of blood.   Oh dear, oh dear! will you just lift up the bed-clothes from my toe; they have settled down upon it like a sack of sand.   No, no, not so!' he exclaimed; 'you will murder me if you do that.'

Oliver, alarmed at the old man's violence, drew back from the bed, and was looking for some excuse for his immediate retreat from the room, when the old man whined out, 'Oh dear, oh dear! it is very hard that I should have no one but you to care for me.   Do speak to your father, and ask him to take the doctor to task for not coming to me before this time of day, and—'

What more he would have said was cut short by the entrance of the gentleman in question.

'Ah, Mr Oliver!' he said, on entering, 'very good of you to pay your old servant a visit.   Well, and how is it with the patient?'

'I am afraid he is very poorly,' said Oliver.

'Poorly!' screamed out the old man; 'I am

mad with pain, and you leave me here till the middle of the day, as if I was nothing better than a dog.'

'You are getting through the day pretty fast,' said the doctor; 'why, it is but just ten o'clock.'

'Well,' retorted the patient; 'then it only wants two hours of the time. And now you are come, what are you going to do for me?'

'Feel your pulse and look at your tongue, and—'

'Feel my pulse and look at my tongue!' cried the old steward. 'What have they to do with my toe? Give me something to ease that or cut it off.'

'Would you like me to try what a little cutting would do?' asked the doctor with assumed gravity, as he took his case of instruments out of his pocket.

'Don't you be a fool,' said the old man. 'Remember I knew you when you were a little chap.'

'Come, come,' said the doctor, 'we must not travel backwards, or I shall have to remind you of some of your odd ways.'

'What odd ways?' retorted the old man fiercely.

'When the gout is gone,' said the doctor, 'I

will answer your question; but now, tell me
how you feel.'

'Very bad,' was the reply.

'But if you will be patient—'

'Patient!' exclaimed the old man, 'I am as
patient as an angel—oh! oh! oh! What are
you about?

'I want to see your foot.'

'Don't touch it! don't touch it! You will
drive me mad.'

'You will alarm the house,' said the doctor.

'And well I may, if you pull me about like a
log of wood.'

'Why, I have not even touched you.'

'But you look as if you would. Birds have
wings to fly away from their enemies, and mice
have holes in which they can run, but there is
no escape from a doctor when he gets a man on
a sick-bed.'

'But we will not call yours a sick-bed. It is
only one of your old attacks, and will soon pass
away. You must get some one to come and sit
with you, and tell you what is going on in the
world; then you will be well again.'

'But where shall I get the some one?'

'I will look out for a man, and he shall bring
you something to take when the pain is very
great.'

' I will have no man of yours here,' said the old steward savagely ; ' you are too much for me as it is. Send your stuff, but don't expect me to keep your messenger.'

' Very well,' said the doctor, after a little more conversation in the same strain had passed between them ; ' it shall be as you wish. Good morning.'

As soon as he was gone, Oliver, who had been looking on with a blanched face while the contest between the doctor and his patient was in progress, said,—

' Do you know, Lea, a thought has just struck me that I have some one who would just suit you. It is my man Jasper. I could spare him for a good part of the day.'

' Jasper ! Why, the fellow would drive me wild.'

' Not if I were to tell him how much you suffer, and beg him to be attentive to you. If you will try him you can send him away again if he does not answer.'

' Without offending you ? '

' Oh yes ; do not think a word about that.'

' Then let him come, sir.'

Bent on his good-natured mission, Oliver left the room, and shortly afterwards a gentle knock was heard at the door.

'Come in,' cried the old steward.

Jasper noiselessly opened the door, and walked softly into the room.

'Why do you come creeping in as if you meant to murder me?' cried the old man.

'Mr Oliver said I was to be sure and not make a noise. What can I do for you, sir?'

'Just keep where you are, and tell me what rascality you have been up to lately.'

'None, sir.'

'That's a lie,' said the old steward, 'or you must be greatly changed within the last few days.'

I think I am a little changed, sir.'

'And what has changed you?'

'I don't know, sir,' said Jasper; 'but I feel something here which I never felt before.'

As he spoke he placed his hand languidly on his left side.

'Why, that's just over your heart.'

'Is it, sir? Then that's why I feel so queer.'

'Heart disease! heart disease!' cried the old steward. 'You must not stop here; you will frighten me to death. Go to the doctor and ask him if it is safe for you to be about alone, and then ask your master to come and

tell me. Go away—go away! You may die
at any moment.'

'No; I am sound enough in health,' said
Jasper. 'It isn't what you think it is.'

'Then what in the world is the matter with
you?'

'Why, you see, sir, Mr Oliver told me
the other day I was getting too old for him,
and since that something has happened to me.'

'Well, what is it?' was the impatient inquiry.
'Have you got another place?'

'No, sir, but Nancy Dicks wants to marry
me, and that has made me queer here,' and
again his hand was placed tenderly on his
heart.

'Now, Jasper!' stormed the old steward,
'if you think you can play off your tricks
upon me because I am a prisoner here, it
won't do; so don't you try it on.'

'But it's all true,' said Jasper thoughtfully.

'Do you mean to tell me that you are going
to marry Nancy Dicks?'

'She wants to marry me, and I'm thinking
about it.'

'Why, she's old enough to be your mother.
If you, you foolish fellow, wish to get married,
why don't you look out for a girl of your own
age?'

'Girls of my age,' said Jasper ruefully, 'unless they are very poor, don't care to look much at me, and if they did, they might not have three hundred pounds of their own to do as they like with as Nancy—'

'Nancy worth three hundred pounds!' cried the old steward, interrupting him; 'you have lost your wits, Jasper.'

'No, sir,' replied Jasper, 'it's only my heart. You know Nancy's mother is dead, and Nancy is to have all her money.'

'All to her? Has she left it all to her?'

'Yes,' replied Jasper, more cheerfully, 'and her business too, and her sisters are to have nothing to do with it.'

'And so you, you young scamp, you think you will marry Nancy?'

'You see, sir, she wants me to, and I have been thinking it would not be right to disappoint her.'

'Why, she is more than half a fool.'

'She says I may have the money and the business if I will have her.'

'And what do your fellows say about it?'

'Oh, I don't care for them,' said Jasper, in a defiant tone.

CHAPTER X.

THE continuance for a week of the old steward's attack of gout proved a sore trial to Jesse. He felt that he was placed in a false position to every one around him. To act in a manner that had even the appearance of dishonesty was foreign to his nature. 'Let me know my duty, and I will, through good report and evil report, endeavour to do it,' was his favourite maxim, and which he strove to keep constantly before him.

His love for Miss Montag was still the all-pervading subject of his thoughts, and how he could work out the problem of her birth became the task even of his dreams. Night and day he meditated upon the best means of escaping from his unpleasant dilemma. His father was still as ever trusting and kind, and it vexed him to his very soul when he thought of the return he was making of his confidence. Again and again he resolved to speak to him, and confessing his love for Miss Montag, throw himself upon his indulgence, but he was as often, by some trifling cause, diverted from his purpose.

'I wish I could share that old man's gout with him,' he thought, ' so that it might shorten the time of his confinement to his room, and get him out for his usual walk, then I might have a chance of obtaining the information I require. I am now like a caged tiger, and can only turn and turn about to no purpose. I cannot stand this much longer. Even Lizzie will see how deficient I am in resolution. Every time I meet her eyes they seem to ask me if I have spoken to my father. I answer " No, but I will speak to him, do not fear," and I believe she does not fear, but like me she is ashamed of our clandestine meetings, which, doubtless, a little open dealing on my part would render unnecessary.'

One morning, on paying a visit to the old steward, he found him so much better that he suggested his getting downstairs once more and seeing some of his old friends.

'I have no friends that care about me.'

'Oh yes, you have ; there is the vicar, Mr

Gordon, he must be an old friend, as you have lived near to each other for so many years.'

'And why should he care for me? I have nothing to give him for his church.'

'Well,' said Jesse, 'as soon as you can get downstairs I shall ask him to pay you a visit. I am glad to see you so much better, but I suppose you must keep quiet for a day or two longer. We will hear what the doctor has to say about it presently.'

He did not stop for further conversation, but, going to his own room and equipping himself for a struggle with briar and bramble, took his gun and left the Hall. He did not inquire for his father or Oliver; nor did he take his usual path to the keeper's house, but, skirting the wood in the opposite direction, reached a path that led through an ornamental part of the ground, where the wood, with its stately elms and acres of underwood, had given place to various kinds of shrubs from all parts of the world.

Was it a mere accident that took him there, and placed him by the side of Miss Montag, on a rustic seat under the foliage of an evergreen oak? Alas, no! By earnest persuasion he had induced her to walk with little Georgie in that particular direction, for the purpose of meeting him, that they might speak freely together of their present situation, after he had told her, as he purposed doing, the main points of what he had heard from the two gentlemen at Brighton.

His patience and his high spirit had alike yielded to the pressure cast upon them. He had resolved not to tell Miss Montag anything of what he had heard until every shadow of doubt had passed away. And here he was now, in the midst of his doubts, about to arrest her attention by a half discovered story, which could do nothing but fill her with anxiety, not only respecting the future, but the past also. While the nobleness of spirit that had made him resolve not to act in any way towards his father, as if he feared to let him look into his heart, had for the time almost deserted him.

But thus far he had not openly transgressed any expressed command of his father, or induced Lizzie to do anything that could bring a blush of shame upon her cheek. Nor had he the slightest intention of doing so. He was as earnest as ever to set himself right with his father, but, in his inexperience, he was approaching a precipice of which he did not even dream, and over which he might fall, without one note of alarm to warn him of his danger.

How would it be if some busy-body had tracked his steps to the bench under the ever-green oak, and carried the news to the ears of Sir Edward? With what confidence could Jesse ever hope to be trusted again, when he had himself shown so little confidence in a kind and indulgent father? Such thoughts had heretofore been present in his mind, but they were there no longer. As he sat by the side of his beloved one, and said funny things to Georgie, who was climbing up on one knee and sliding down from the other, he was one of the happiest of the happy, and was only recalled to the business in hand by Lizzie observing, 'You said you had something to tell me when you proposed that I should meet you here.'

'Yes; and now if you will listen,' replied Jesse, 'I will tell you, not all that I could wish, but all that I am at present able.'

But instead of quietly listening, she started suddenly from her seat and clasped the child in her arms. A gun had been discharged within a few paces of the spot, and she expected every moment to see Sir Edward standing before them. But she was happily soon undeceived. It was only Dixon, who, in answer to Jesse's inquiry of what he had fired at, said it was only a weasel, and he believed he had settled him.

'Are you here alone?' asked Jesse.

'No, sir; Sir Edward and Mr Oliver are close at hand.'

'Take away! take away! Georgie don't like weasels!' screamed the child.

'There is none to hurt you here,' said Jesse, 'but perhaps you would be quite as safe at home. Please tell Smith that I shall be round with him at the appointed time. He is not with my father, is he?' he added to Dixon.

'No; I think he is waiting for you at home, sir,' replied Dixon.

As he finished speaking they were confronted by Sir Edward and Oliver.

The father looked surprised, while Oliver said, 'Hallo, Jesse! what are you doing here? I thought you were out with Smith; he told us just now that he was waiting for you.'

'You came round this way by chance,' said Sir Edward.

Jesse hesitated for a moment, and then said, 'No, father, I did not.'

Miss Montag, with the child in her arms, was in the act of moving away when her step was arrested by Sir Edward, who said, 'Stop one moment, I will not detain you long.' He then having directed Oliver and Dixon to go on to the wood, continued, 'It may have been mere chance that has brought you two young people together here ; but, so or not, I trust it is the last time, as it is the first, that I shall find you thus together.   I think I need not remind you that we are living in a very censorious world.'

' Father,' said Jesse, ' the world may say what it pleases ; I care not for it.   But if your finding us here alone offends you I am very sorry.'

' It would rather grieve than offend me,' replied Sir Edward, ' if I thought my son Jesse could act an unworthy part.   Do not let me detain you, Miss Montag.   If I find it necessary, I will speak to you alone at some future time.'

Miss Montag, covered with confusion, was about to make an attempt to reply, when Jesse interposed and said, ' It is for me to explain. Go ; go, Lizzie.   I will tell my father how it happened that we met here.'   As soon as she was gone he turned to his father and said, ' Is it strange that I should love her ? '

' Love her ! ' repeated Sir Edward.

' Yes,' replied Jesse ; ' love her most truly.'

' If I do not think it strange to hear you say so,' replied Sir Edward, ' I think it is most unfortunate.   What have I done to you, Jesse, that you should have treated me thus? In what have I shown a want of confidence in you that you have shown you have so little in me?'

'Father,' replied Jesse, 'you have spoken the same words my conscience has been saying to me ever since my return from Brighton.'

'And why have you not listened to it and acted on its prompting?' asked Sir Edward.

'I have listened to it,' replied Jesse passionately, 'and have resolved to open my heart to you, but I have waited till I could show you that Miss Montag is worthy of all the love I could bestow upon her.'

'This is indeed most unfortunate,' said Sir Edward. 'Jesse,' he continued, in a broken voice, 'you speak of opening your heart to me. My dear boy, it should never have been closed. Ask yourself. Is it the return you should have made me? When did you ever find my heart closed to you, when I thought you needed advice or counsel? How can you excuse yourself for the injury you have done yourself and me?'

'I have no excuse to offer,' replied Jesse, 'in loving Miss Montag. I do not feel that I have committed a crime. If I have, it is one I could not avoid. I loved her before I knew it myself. How then could I ask you if I might love her ? Do the birds in spring-time ask permission to sing, or the flowers to burst into blossom when wooed by the summer sun ? '

'You are growing a little romantic, Jesse,' said his father, 'and I cannot follow you in your flights of fancy, but if you can for a few minutes act as the reasonable being I have hitherto hoped you were, we will, as we stroll homewards, look at the affair as it will appear to the world, should it come to its knowledge.'

'Hang the world!' cried Jesse. 'I do not care how it appears in its eyes.'

'Well, then, to come nearer home. Let me say how it appears to me.'

'I am very sorry that I did not speak to you when I first made the discovery.'

'And I am very sorry too,' said his father; 'but come, let us look at the case as it now stands before us. Who are you and who is Miss Montag ? Will your position permit you to take a wife from so low a grade ? Supposing a person under similar circum-stances to yourself were married, would he like, when he entered on the active business of life, to be looked upon as a single man, or one who dared not take his wife into the society of his friends ? '

'I do not know such a person,' said Jesse.

'And I trust I do not,' replied Sir Edward; 'but tell me, Jesse, how long has the present state of things existed?'

'If you mean how long I have loved Miss Montag I cannot say, for I do not know myself, but if you only mean how long it is since it found expression in words, I have to go back to a few days before I left Brighton.'

'Do I understand you to say you met Miss Montag at Brighton?'

'Yes,' replied Jesse, 'and there discovered that my love was reciprocated, and, but for an incident that occurred there that day, on my return I should have come direct to you and told you all.'

'And may I ask you to tell me the nature of the incident that could thus thrust itself between our hearts, and make you treat me as a stranger?'

'It is nothing wrong,' said Jesse, 'but at present I cannot tell you, as it would be useless or worse.'

'What! still doubtful of your best friend, Jesse?' said his father very mournfully.

'Father,' cried Jesse, 'I am not doubtful. I have unbounded confidence in your goodness and judgment, but you must know that

if our meeting here has been a surprise to you'
it has not been less so to me. To - morrow
I proposed coming to you and confessing my
love, even though you might have answered
me with a curse on my folly.'

'A curse on your folly ?' said Sir Edward.

'I should have felt your censure as a curse,'
said Jesse.

'Then you would have judged me harshly; but
come, let us endeavour to understand each other.
Whatever course I may deem it my duty to take
in this painful affair, you must not look upon me
as an enemy. We will say no more about it at
present, but follow the counsel of the old adage
—sleep upon it. I only ask you to give me
your word that you will not see Miss Montag
again until I have spoken to her, and that, I
promise you, shall be early to-morrow morning.'

'That is repaying me in my own coin,' said
Jesse, with a faint smile, 'but I must not
complain.'

'And for the present, as far as words are
concerned, we will treat it as an old forgotten
story. Were you not to meet Smith this
morning ?'

'Yes,' replied Jesse, 'but I think I must not
go to his house to-day, or perchance my word
will be broken.'

'I will go with you,' said his father. 'Probably we shall meet him on the way. He
knows nothing of what you have told me, I
trust ?'

'No, nothing,' replied Jesse.

They had gone but a few steps when they
saw Oliver with Smith and Dixon in the distance coming towards them. On meeting they
learnt that Oliver and Dixon had come upon a
trail of what appeared to them evidence that
strangers had been upon the spot a short time
previously, and they were then taking Smith
to the place for a closer investigation.

True to his promise, Sir Edward was early
the next morning at the keeper's house, and to
his great satisfaction found Miss Montag there
alone. Smith he learnt was out with his men,
and his wife, after having sent off her elder
children to school, had taken Georgie with her
to the village to do a little shopping.

Sir Edward commenced the conversation by
saying,—

'I am glad to find you alone, Miss Montag,
as I wish to speak privately to you upon a
subject in which we are both doubtless much
interested.'

Miss Montag, surprised at the gentleness of
his manner, endeavoured to answer, but her

tongue would not obey her will, and perforce she remained silent. She felt the hour had come she had looked forward to with so much dread, and with it a thousand regrets for the past and of fears for the future.

'Do not think,' continued Sir Edward, 'that I have come to you under the influence of unreasonable anger. Since I saw you yesterday, I have heard from my son that he is chiefly to blame for your, to say the least of it, indiscreet meeting in the shrubbery. But I think you must know that it is very necessary you should be careful of your reputation, and avoid placing yourself in an equivocal position.'

'I am very sorry, Sir Edward,' said Miss Montag, 'that I have offended you,' at length finding her voice, and bursting into tears.

'I may repeat to you,' rejoined Sir Edward, 'that I told my son yesterday I am not so much offended as I am grieved. I do not wish to say an unkind word to either of you, but I must speak out, and plainly. I will not charge you with wilful deception. I trust that of which I have to complain has arisen from thoughtlessness rather than wickedness. You are well aware of the terms on which you are living here. The secret of your childhood, as far as we could follow it, has not been kept from you.

You know that the late Lady Harewood for years indulged the hope that she would be able to unravel the mystery of your first appearance in the park, but she died without making the desired discovery. The charge she left me, I think you must be aware, I have not shrunk from. Neither your education, nor that of your brother, has been neglected ; and I am happy to say your brother has fulfilled my most sanguine expectation of what I looked for from him ; and although I may not have appeared to take so much interest in your welfare, I have been no unobservant witness of your conduct ; and until yesterday—'

'Please, Sir Edward,' broke in Miss Montag, 'before you condemn me—'

'You must listen to what I have to say to you,' said Sir Edward, interrupting her in turn. 'I say until yesterday not a single doubt crossed my mind respecting the position you would occupy at no distant time, either as housekeeper to your brother or the wife of one of my tenants.'

'You have always been very good to me,' sobbed the poor girl; 'but I did not wish to leave Mrs Smith.'

'Nor should I have wished to hurry you away,' said Sir Edward, 'if the present unhappy incident had not occurred; but you must be aware how very different the case is now. You are still young, and my son has not yet commenced his career in life. I am sorry to be obliged to speak so plainly to you, but you have left me no choice. Neither of you know enough of the world, or of your own hearts, to be left to follow your present inclinations. I will not again repeat the obligations you are under to me, but in consideration of them I must beg you to consent to what, after mature deliberation, I have to propose to you.'

'I will do anything,' replied Miss Montag, 'that does not carry with it the appearance of my having wilfully deceived you.'

'You admit you have deceived me?'

'Oh! yes,' said Miss Montag, 'but how unwillingly you cannot know, nor can I tell you. From a child I have looked upon Mr Jesse almost as a god. He has always been so good and kind to me. But when I found I was thinking of him more than I thought I ought to do, I tried to keep away from him, and cure myself of my folly. With that view I seized upon the opportunity that I had of going to Brighton; but, alas! I took his dear image in my heart with me, and when chance brought us together there, the truth burst involuntarily from my eyes.'

'Poor child!' said Sir Edward, 'I may pity you, but I must not let my feelings overweigh my judgment. I sought you this morning to speak more harshly to you than I have done, but I must not leave you in any doubt respecting the future. You cannot remain here. I will immediately find a fitting place for you to go to, where you will be well cared for. But on this condition only, that you give me your solemn promise that you will take no means to let my son know where you are; and further, if he should discover the place of your retirement, you will not agree to any proposal he may make to you without first consulting me.'

'And may I not see him before I make this promise?'

'No,' replied Sir Edward; 'you must give it me at once,'

'And must I go away without seeing him?'

'Yes; unless you are content to see him in my presence this morning. I do not wish to appear harsh, but I must do my best to guard you against your own rashness.'

'I am in your hands,' said Miss Montag; 'and what can I do but trust to your generosity.'

'Then you will make immediate preparation for your departure to London, where I will leave you with a person who I know will treat you kindly until I can communicate with your brother at Bath, and some permanent provision can be made for you. As you will require to take your luggage with you, I will send the carriage for it. Be ready by two o'clock and you shall see my son before you leave Woodfield.'

Returning to the Hall, Sir Edward did not feel himself so much reconciled to the duty that had been forced upon him as he could have wished. Thoughts of his Oxford days came back upon him, dragging after them a train of reflections which had their centre in the idea that, if he had been as open in the expression of his love for Edith, how much vexation and trouble he might have escaped. These thoughts and reflections did not, however, cause him to change his purpose.

Summoning Jesse to come to him in the library, he told him in few words what he had done, and what he proposed to do. He did not speak as he had done the day before, in a tone of expostulation and persuasion, but rather as a parent commanding a child. His heart had been so nearly touched by the artless confession of the two young people of their love for each other, that he dared not use more gentle words lest the bright eyes of Jesse should put him from his purpose, and thus render the exercise of his judgment vain.

Jesse, having sent one pleading look to his father, stood before him with drooping head, and eyes fixed on the ground, listening attentively to the deliberate words that fell upon his ear. When the address was finished, he replied with a sigh,—'It is for you, father, to dictate terms to me, and I do not disguise from myself that I have been very foolish. If I had acted in accordance with the wish of her of whose love I hope at some future time to prove myself worthy, I should have come direct to you, and openly confessed that which has come before you under such suspicious circumstances. I must now abide by your decision, and I do it the more readily since you will permit me to clasp her hand in mine, and look once more into her eyes before you part us—shall I say for ever?'

Sir Edward, with all his knowledge of the world, and the intricate working of the human heart, was taken a little aback by what appeared to him the cool manner in which Jesse had listened to words whose import was, he believed, so little in accordance with his desire. For a moment or two he looked suspiciously at his son. Was he making some mental reservation in his ready promise not to take any means of following Miss Montag to her retirement. No, that could not be. The whole bearing of Jesse forbad the supposition. Honesty beamed from his eyes, and his words had a ring of truth in them, not to be doubted.

'Have I then,' he thought, 'unnecessarily frightened myself? Is the wound not so deep as I have feared it was? If such is happily the case, we may soon get back again to our normal condition.' While thus comforting himself with delusive hopes, he had missed one essential element in the case before him for the formation of a correct judgment upon it.

He had looked upon Jesse's confession of love as from a boy, who had seen too little of the world for it to make a lasting impression, but he had expected him to fire up against making any promise about his feelings which he had not been able to control. To say that he must be trusted as a man, or he should feel as a slave ashamed of himself, and much more of the same kind. He did not know that his son's confession was only a part of the desire that filled his heart. Even his love appeared to fall into the background, in comparison with his

ardent resolve to trace out the parentage of
Miss Montag and her brother.

He would have explained this to his father,
had he not felt that by doing so he might raise
up obstacles to perplex and annoy him. He felt
he must be alone, and for a time at least work
in secret. So much was this the case, that he was
rather pleased than otherwise that Miss Montag
was to be sent away. That he could find her
when her presence would be required, he had
no doubt. If he could establish the family
relationship between her family and his, he
thought all opposition to their meeting again
would cease, and, in the meantime, he knew she
would be well cared for.

He rode in the carriage with his father to the
keeper's house, where they found all in readi-
ness for the departure. Mrs Smith bustled
about making herself very useful, and apparently not over curious. She knew perfectly
well what was taking place, though Miss Montag
had been silent on the main point. A hint from
Dixon of the meeting in the shrubbery yesterday, and her own observation, told her that Sir
Edward had taken the matter in hand, and was
in the act of separating the lovers. She was
thrown a little out of her reckoning at first when
she saw Jesse with his father, but when she saw

the carriage drive off and leave him behind, she thought Sir Edward might, good-naturedly, have allowed him to be present to take a last farewell.

A few words only passed between Jesse and Miss Montag. She looked earnestly at him, as if she would ask him if he had nothing more to tell her about something he was on the point of doing yesterday; but he did not pay any special attention to her silent appeal. With a warm pressure of the hand, and a God bless you, after a few loving words had been whispered between them they parted, Miss Montag taking her place in the carriage by the side of Sir Edward, and Jesse, cap in hand, standing by the door until the horses were in motion.

'Now,' thought Jesse, as he strode away to the seat in the shrubbery, that witnessed the surprise of yesterday,' the coast is clear for my work, and I must immediately set earnestly about it. If it is necessary, I will ransack Germany until I find the place of which the two gentlemen spoke. It is a long time, no doubt, to look back upon, but still there must be many yet alive who have some recollection of the incident I am so anxious to investigate.

'If I can only see the old steward once on his

legs again ; what with a little prompting from my father and Mr Gordon, it will go hard with me, though I fail in getting the whole truth from him, if I do not get some information that will make my search comparatively easy.'

CHAPTER XI.

THUS Sir Edward Harewood was fairly off on what he thought a mission of mercy to save two young people from an entanglement which had no promise of good in it, but a great deal of mischief. The girl by his side, for aught he knew to the contrary, might be the daughter of a princess, or, on the other hand, she might be the child of a common beggar, or something worse. What could be looked forward to from a connection with such a person ? What but worry and anxiety.

As these thoughts passed through his mind, a tone of satisfaction overspread his countenance as he secretly complimented himself on the decision with which he had acted as soon as he knew of its necessity. Could he at that time have seen what was taking place at Marseilles, it is very doubtful if his satisfaction would have been so pleasantly expressed. He might have

felt that the scandal of a baronet's son marrying
a poor orphan girl would have been as nothing
to that trial which was being prepared for him
to encounter.

Lyson had received an answer from his
father, which contained a few words put in
secretly by his sisters, in which the name of Sir
Edward Harewood was mentioned in connection with Edith's in no very complimentary
terms. That filled up the cup of his wrath.
Though alone at the time, he stamped angrily
about the room, and swore he would be
revenged, forgetful that he had, by his own
misconduct, banished his wife from his house.

'A pretty thing,' he stormed, 'that I should
be driven into exile from my wife by his
machinations with but a poor pittance to live
upon, while he has everything the heart of man
can desire, and yet is not content but he must
rob me of my wife. Yes, he must play with
her, flatter her, and be again with her as the
companion of her childhood, but armed with
the knowledge and vigour of a man. And have
I known this and borne with it in silence?
Yes, coward that I am, I have. But I will
bear with it no longer. If it costs me my
head I will be revenged. He shall suffer and
pay till we are quits. But when that will be

the gods only know, so long and black a score have I to work off against him.'

In his mind he dipped his pen in gall, and set to work to write to Mr Cresswell. He would let him understand that he should not keep his wife away from him. He would desire that she should be sent out to him at once. His forbearance in not having done so before, had been used simply as an instrument of oppression, and he would bear with it no longer.

That he had, through the roguery of his dependents in Paris, been deprived of his appointment, and sent out a wanderer amongst strangers. That, weary and exhausted, he wanted rest, and, however displeasing it might be to some people, he would seek it in his native land, and amidst the beloved and dearly remembered scenes of his youth.

This, and a great deal more in the same strain, he committed to paper, but he did not send his letter. Circum returned from his journey of investigation, and a gentler and more subtle mode of proceeding took the place of the aggressive one he had been preparing for.

Circum reported that he had learnt, partly from his own personal observation, and partly from intelligence he had received from his

friends, that the girl he had assisted the son of
the late Sir Henry Harewood to marry, lived
for some time in a cottage near Heilbron, where
she was visited by her husband, and where two
children were afterwards born, a boy and a girl.
That her husband having disappeared and her
aunt died, she fell into pecuniary difficulties and
was obliged to sell off her goods and remove to
another village, from which, after struggling
for a while with adverse fortune, she went
away in the direction of Manheim, where he
had lost all trace of her.

'Then your journey has been in vain,' said
Lyson gloomily, 'and my ten pounds spent to
little purpose? What do you propose to do
now? Give it up as a lost game?'

'By no means,' said Circum.

'But you tell me,' said Lyson, 'that you
have exhausted all your means of discovery.'

'No, no,' said Circum, 'you alarm yourself
too readily. The game is not up yet, for I
have found a trump card or two. I know the
boy we want was alive with his sister, under
the care of his mother, who, to my mind, when
she was last seen in Germany, was making her
way towards the Rhine.'

'To drown herself and her children,' said
Lyson sarcastically.

'No,' replied Circum ;- 'but according to a theory I have formed in my mind, to get on board one of the river steamers, and cross over to England in search of her runaway husband. What took place when she discovered he was dead it is hard to say. She may have looked in at Woodcome Hall, and been pensioned off by your good friend there, or failing that, she may have found shelter in some out - of - the - way place, and been kept quiet by the old servant or some one else interested in the good name of the family, at any rate, until we have carried our search in that direction, I shall not be satisfied.'

'But the means,' said Lyson ; 'the means, where are they to come from ?'

'Have you written to your father?' asked Circum.

'Yes, and got his answer ;. and written to Cresswell.'

'And sent your letter ?'

'No, I have it here ; I have just finished it you may look at it if you like.'

Circum having hastily run his eye over the letter, said,—

'You wrote this when you were angry ; a bad thing to do. You should never write to

a friend when you are out of temper. A man
at such a time is apt to say things which he is
soon after very sorry for.'

' But I was provoked.'

' The very reason why you should not have
touched your pen. When you write, let your
face be covered with smiles, no matter whether
they are real or not ; the effect your words will
produce on the reader will be the same. Besides,
anger is the last stage of a quarrel. Angry
men shoot and kill their best friends. We are
far away from that point. A soft tongue and
gentle words are what we most require now.
My proposal to you is that I set out at once
for London, from whence I can work my way
into the country, and as the old saying has it,
kill two birds with one stone.'

' How ? I don't understand,' said Lyson.

' You must not take offence,' replied Circum, 'if
I remind you that I think I have heard you couple
your wife's name with that of a certain baronet.'

' Yes, curse him ! ' cried Lyson.

' No anger,' said Circum ; ' we must be very
cool, and before we attempt to open our mine,
look a little about us to find a tool or two for
our work. I need not tell you that suspicion
in a court of justice goes for nothing unless it
is supported by unquestionable evidence. Tell

me, what do you know of your wife's playful
tricks? Have you witnesses to say they have
seen so-and-so?'

' I know what my sisters say.'

' And what they have seen. No, no. I am
afraid you cannot say that. Your wife and the
baronet did not go to the roof of the house to
exhibit themselves, as we read in an old book
a certain man did years ago. They are too
modern for that, and if you were to charge
them with wrong-doing from the hearsay
accounts of your sisters, they would laugh in
your face, and instead of your opening a rich
mine you would effectually bury it beneath a
mass of unprofitable rubbish. Let me go into
their neighbourhood, as you lately proposed I
should, that I may make sure of anything that
is to be found out, or can be invented, to further
your views.'

' But where is the money to come from for
the journey?'

' You are not so hard up that you cannot get
a few pounds for such a purpose.'

' I suppose,' said Lyson, ' I must lend out
my watch again?'

' It will not be for long,' was the reply; ' we
have the trump cards in our hands, and we will
play them out very carefully.'

While Sir Edward Harewood was with his charge on his way to London, and Jesse was mapping out the future in his mind as he sat on the rustic seat in the shrubbery, made sacred to him by the events of yesterday, Oliver found himself master at the Hall, and as such, was called upon to exercise its authority. Shortly after his father had left, and before Jesse's return, Jasper came to him, and said,—

'Mr Lea wants to see you in his room directly, sir.'

'I am just going out with my sister,' replied Oliver; 'tell him I will see him as soon as I come back.'

'And I want to speak to you too,' said Jasper.

'Well, what is it? make haste and tell me. I must not keep my sister and Miss Gordon waiting, you know.'

'You said I might leave my place when I liked, sir.'

'Yes, I know I did; I told you my father said so.'

'I wish to leave this afternoon, sir.'

'This afternoon!' said Oliver, 'that is rather sudden, and you know I lent you to Lea; I cannot let you go to-day.'

'Then there will be a noise in the village,' said Jasper.

'What do you mean? Do be quick and tell me.'

'Nancy says I must go to church with her to-morrow.'

'Well, what is there to prevent you? Do you not generally go to church on a Sunday?'

'Yes, but Nancy says she will have me go from her house with her, and that I must leave my place to-day.'

'Oh dear,' said Oliver, 'then I suppose she means to be master. What is to be done? I am sure I do not know. I must speak to my father before I can say you may go, and he is from home. Why did you not tell me of this before he left?'

'I didn't know Nancy would want me then,' replied Jasper.

'Well,' said Oliver, 'you go to Mr Lea, and tell him I am gone to the village, but that I will come and see him very soon. Stop there with him until I come, and then I can tell you what Charlotte thinks of your going to-day, and perhaps I shall see Jesse, and I can tell you what he says too.'

'Well,' said the old steward, as Jasper re-entered his room, 'did you tell Mr Oliver I wished to see him directly?'

'Yes,' replied Jasper, 'and I was to inform

you that he is gone to the village, and will come to you as soon as he gets back.'

' You impudent rascal,' cried the old steward, ' you did not say I wished to see him directly ? '

' I did, though,' said Jasper, ' and I told him too, that I wanted to leave my place this afternoon.'

' You unfeeling brute ! ' exclaimed the old steward. ' If I were able to get up from my chair I would put my stick about your back.'

' Then it is a good thing for me that you are not able.'

' Just when I have taught you to be useful to me, you must want to run away and get married. What can a boy like you want with a wife ? Who put the nonsense into your head, did you say ? Oh, I remember, that fool of a Nancy Dicks.'

' She is not my wife yet, sir,' said Jasper, ' but you had better not call her names even now.'

' And why not, pray, you little jackanapes ? '

' Why, because if you do, you may expect a visit from her, and she may perhaps take upon herself to shake a little explanation out of you.'

' I will have you both sent to the treadmill ! ' cried Lea, and in the excitement of the moment he arose from his seat and took a step towards the offender, with his stick in his upraised hand, when, unfortunately for him, his long dressing-gown got under his feet, and instead of his stick falling on the shoulders of Jasper, it fell from his hand to the floor, as he staggered forward on the point of toppling over after it, when his attendant caught him in his arms, and pressed him back again into his chair.

'What did you do that for?' exclaimed the old steward, puffing and blowing like a steam-engine; 'you nearly threw me down.'

'Did I, indeed?' said Jasper; 'well, now, I thought I saved you from falling, but some people have strange notions about what happens to them.'

'Hark! what noise is that?' said the old steward.

'It is Nancy, I think, inquiring for me.'

'Then go out to her; go out directly.'

'Shall I tell her you say she is a fool.'

'No, no!' screamed the old man; 'go out to her directly, and take her to one of the men, and give her a glass of ale, and tell him I said she was to have it. Oh dear, oh dear! how I am worried. Everybody seems to take a pleasure to see me suffer. There, go, go, I hear her again. Why don't you go?'

' Then I may leave my place this afternoon ? '

' Leave your place and go to the—' He did not finish the sentence, a twitch in his toe, caused by his late exertion, caused him to scream out, ' There is the gout coming back again ! Was there ever such an unfortunate wretch as I am ? '

In the midst of his complaints, Jesse, having returned from the shrubbery, entered the room.

' Oh, Mr Jesse,' he continued, ' you are come just in time to save my life, though perhaps even you will not think it worth saving. That rascal of a boy had driven me almost wild.'

' I am sorry for that. What has he done ? '

' And Mr Oliver, I sent for him, and he would not come to me.'

' Perhaps,' said Jesse gently, ' he could not. You know he has undertaken duties in the parish with his sister.'

' And where could he find any one in the parish worse than I am, or who wanted him more ? '

' Can I supply his place ? ' asked Jesse.

' If you had been here a little sooner you might. That rascal of a boy has gone away and left me just when I stand most in need of him.'

' Do you mean Jasper ? '

'Yes, who else should I mean? He was to stop with me as long as I was confined in this wretched room, and just when I have taught him to be useful he has run away. I wanted Mr Oliver to come and tell him he should not go. But nobody cares to do anything for me.'

'I shall be glad to stop with you,' said Jesse, 'and have a little talk with you about old times, before you were subject to this terrible gout.'

'Don't say a word about old times. I can remember nothing while I am shut up here. Do just put this cushion up for me. Oh dear! that rascal of a boy, he will be the death of me. To run away just as he was becoming useful. I hope he will soon grow old, and get as bad as I am, that I do.'

In this manner the old steward went on complaining during the hour Jesse spent with him, vainly endeavouring to gain some information from him, that he might be quite satisfied that he was the confidential servant he had heard the gentleman speaking of at the hotel in Brighton.

It was late in the evening before Sir Edward returned from London, and as he afterwards sat in the drawing-room with his family, he did not feel that his proceedings during the day had been of a clear and far-seeing character. The idea that had crossed his mind when speaking to Jesse, that his heart was not so seriously affected as he had feared it was, grew in strength with the passing time.

Jesse was ready with his usual cheerfulness to greet him on his return. He did not appear over-curious to inquire respecting the incidents of the day, or to what particular part of London he had been.

'He cannot be so desperately in love with the girl,' thought the father, 'or he would not be so easily satisfied. I might have saved myself the weariness of my journey since, if I now judge correctly, a sharp word or two from me would have brought the young people to their senses, and ended the affair with a few tears and empty protestations. Still, if I have erred from over-caution, my error has been on the right side, and the cure I have aimed at may be the sooner effected.'

The name of the old steward arose in a conversation between Oliver and Charlotte, when Sir Edward, who sat near them, said,—

'You remind me that I have forgotten to inquire for the poor old fellow. How has he been during the day?'

'Very bad, indeed!' said Charlotte, 'judging from what Oliver has been telling me.'

' I am sorry for that,' said Sir Edward.

' I am inclined to think,' observed Jesse, ' that he makes the most of his troubles, or that he has a fondness of creating them for his own amusement. I sat with him for an hour to-day, and strove very hard to get his thoughts away from himself in the present ; but I could in no-wise succeed.'

' I did the same,' said Oliver ; ' and I asked him to tell me some of his old stories ; but he could think of nothing but his gout and Jasper, who, I forgot to tell you, papa, left my service to-day.'

' Poor, silly fellow ! ' observed Charlotte, ' I hear he is going to marry that half-witted body, Nancy Dicks.'

' I tried,' said Oliver, ' to persuade him not to leave me to-day ; but he said he must, for Nancy would have him go to church with her to-morrow.'

' Rather an odd couple,' observed Sir Edward.

' Poor old Lea is almost crazy about it,' said Oliver.

' How can it affect him ? ' asked Sir Edward.

' He seems to have grown in his strange way attached to Jasper, and does not like to part with him,' said Charlotte.

' I asked him,' said Jesse, ' to tell me some of

his travelling stories, but, like Oliver, I could
not get him to speak one word on the subject.
His vocabulary seemed confined to "Jasper,"
"rascal," and "gout."'

'He could tell you many amusing stories, if
he chose,' said Charlotte ; and then to her father
she said, ' I have been talking to Oliver about
some of his adventures,—and am I not right,
papa, in saying you told me that he had
written accounts of journeys ? '

' Yes,' replied Sir Edward ; 'when I was
speaking to him once about something that
occurred to me when I was on the Continent—
the full particulars of which I could not remember—he said he always kept notes of what
happened when he was travelling with my
uncle.'

' And did you ever see any of them ? ' broke
in Grace.

' No,' replied Sir Edward ; but when I
employed him on a certain mission, I asked
him on his return to write me out a short
account of it.'

' And did he do so ? ' asked Charlotte.

' Yes,' replied Sir Edward ; ' but it is a long
time since, and relates to an affair which is too
old to be interesting now.'

' Oh, do tell me what it was about,' cried

Grace. ' I do so like to hear old stories, particularly when I know the story-teller.'

' But the account I spoke of,' said Sir Edward,
' was not a story.'

' Well, papa,' said Grace, ' it must have been
something interesting, or you would not have
required a written account of it. Do, pray, let
me see it. If you will not, I shall dream of it all
through the night, and I am afraid I shall think
of my dream while I am at church to-morrow.'

Jesse, who had been very busily employed
looking over a large atlas while the conversation
was going on, apparently giving his whole attention to the subject before him, when his ears
were eagerly drinking in every word that floated
through the air. Sir Edward looked at him,
and seeing how little interest he was taking in
what was passing, said to Grace,—

' The paper you so much wish to see is that
which he wrote after his last visit to Germany.'

' That was when he went for poor mamma,'
said Charlotte, ' to make some inquiry about
the children she had so kindly taken under her
protection.'

' Oh, do let us have it, papa,' cried Grace ; ' I
should like to know all he learnt about them.'

' I can tell you that in one word,' said Sir
Edward.

'Yes, papa,' said Grace.

'Nothing!' continued Sir Edward.

'Indeed, papa!' said Grace, a little confused.

'Yes,' continued her father—'nothing; and the paper contains only his account of his journeying from place to place, and the obstacles he met with,—as I have said, all for nothing. You will not care for such a story as that, will you?'

'Only just let me see it, and I will tell you, papa. I think I have read about wolves eating children in Germany, and perhaps I shall find something like it there.'

'Well,' said her father, 'since you are so very curious—if Charlotte will take my keys and go to the library, she will find a sealed packet in the top drawer on the left hand of my writing-table, marked, "Lea's Journey to Germany."'

'Oh, Charlotte!' cried Grace, 'do make haste; I am burning to see it! May I go with her?'

'No,' replied her father, putting his hand on her arm; your little fingers would be too busy there.'

'Oh, papa, how can you say so?' rejoined Grace.

Until Charlotte's return Jesse sat looking at the atlas, but when he saw the packet fairly in the room all his seeming indifference to what

was passing vanished in a moment ; and as Sir
Edward was breaking the seal, he approached
nearer to him, saying as he did so,—

'I had no idea that you had any such paper
in your possession.'

'It contains no secrets,' remarked his father,
'and will, I think, scarcely repay any one for its
perusal. I put it away, as you see it, to please
your mother, and I have thought little of it
since, unless when I chanced to open the drawer
where Charlotte found it.'

'There is not much of it,' said Grace.

'And what there is, if I remember rightly, is
not very interesting,' rejoined her father.

'When all my good friends,' said Jesse, 'have
satisfied themselves with looking it over I will
subject it to a little criticism, that I may form
a few questions upon it to enable me to go
earnestly into the subject with the writer on
some idle or rainy day.'

CHAPTER XII.

GRACE occupied her place in the family pew the next morning at church, with her mind freed from the anxiety that had threatened to disturb her respecting the sealed packet, containing Lea's account of his last visit to Germany. She had not found the subject or the manner in which it was treated very interesting.

Soon after she had taken her seat in church, her usual quiet demeanour when there underwent a considerable change. The pew in which she sat was one of the old-fashioned, high ones, and she was so placed that her back was to the porch from whence there arose a great clattering of nailed boots and shoes on the flags and a buzzing noise of voices, as if some one was putting in order a procession, each separate member of which had a will of its own, and was endeavouring to use it, not in taking the appointed place, but in selecting one according to its own fancy.

To add to her awakened curiosity Grace heard, or fancied she heard, the buzz at the porch spread through the congregation over the whole church. She rose to her feet, but the provoking high pew prevented her from seeing more than what only tended to increase her curiosity. After standing on tiptoe on the hassock for a moment she turned round, and despite of the frowns of her sister Charlotte, placed her knees on the seat and her hands on the back of the pew, and thus gained a position where she could command a view of the porch and the people who were hustling and jostling one another in it.

The most prominent figure of the group, though by no means the tallest, was Nancy Dicks; her mourning thrown off, and decked out in the most elaborate style. If the materials of her dress were not of the best of their kind, they were the brightest and most showy. She did not, however, appear to have been at much trouble to harmonise her colours, but as a grand display was her object, that might be easily accounted for.

Her bonnet, which not only covered her head,

raised itself on high over her red face, with two
wing-like flaps spreading out on each side, and
surmounted by bunches of artificial roses of red,
pink and yellow. A white muslin dress in-
closed her sturdy form, made in the height of
the fashion, but reaching to a point a little
above the top of her boots, and ornamented
with bows of ribbon, of all the hues of the
rainbow, before and behind. Her boots shone
with their highest polish, and formed a fine
finish to the red stockings above. Over her
shoulders was carelessly thrown a long, white
muslin scarf, which on a more interesting occasion was to do duty as a veil.

With the energy with which she had often
put her mother's horse in the shafts of the cart,
she was seen grasping first one and then
another of her four companions, dressed as
nearly like herself as hand could dress them, to
force them into their proper places.

'You are making yourself quite hot,' whispered a friendly voice in her ear.

'These are my bridesmaids,' rejoined Nancy,
'and I'm just showing them how they are to
come into the church with me when I am
married. We have put off our mourning for
the wedding, but we shall wear it again
afterwards. Now, Jasper, where is your

father ? Oh, here you are, all right, and in we go.'

All the ladies, with the exception of Nancy, seemed a little abashed when they saw the eyes of the assembled congregation fixed upon them. But Nancy had come to show herself off to the world, and she was well pleased with the notice the world bestowed upon her, and to see that every face was smiling that met her gaze.

The gay party were scarcely seated when Mr Gordon and his curate entered from the vestry. Many eyes no doubt furtively wandered from the book before them to Nancy, but no one, save the very young and giddy, appeared to take any special notice of her or her friends until the ending of the reading of the second lesson, when Mr Gordon said, ' I publish the banns of marriage between Jasper Gotley and Nancy Jemima Jenkinson Dicks ! '

No sooner had the name of Dicks escaped from the vicar's mouth than there was a sudden clatter in a corner of the church, and a loud whisper of ' Now, now, now is the time,' when the two sisters of Nancy started to their feet, and the eldest cried out in a stern voice, ' I forbid the banns ! '

Eager eyes for the moment were turned in the direction from whence the sound came, but save Nancy, who said loudly enough to be heard by many, 'Oh, that's you, is it Betsey? but it won't do;' no one uttered a word.

Then all eyes turned to the vicar, who said, 'The person who has just spoken will come to the vestry after the service is over and state her reason for what she has said.' He then continued the service to the close as if nothing unusual had occurred. He did not, however, carry the congregation entirely with him, and it is very questionable if many of those who were present could, an hour after the sermon was concluded, have given any very satisfactory account of it.

The vestry of the church was of a tolerable size, but had it been ten times as large it would not have sufficed to hold the half of those who rushed towards it immediately the service was over; and it was not until the clerk had reminded the throng that there was no admittance there except on business, that the curious ones could be induced to withdraw from before the door.

The two elder sisters were, as a matter of course, admitted, but there was some little hesitation about the introduction of Nancy and her party, until the vicar, seeing that there would most likely be an unseemly noise on the outside of the church if she was not admitted, ordered her to come in.

'Now, Miss Betsey,' cried Nancy, as soon as she had passed the threshold, 'what have you got to say agin my banns?'

'Hush, hush!' said the vicar, 'you must not talk here. If you are not quiet I must have you sent out again.'

'You just hold your tongue, Nancy,' whispered Jasper. 'I know what to do if they stop us here.'

'But they can't,' retorted Nancy.

'Now, Mrs Striply,' said the vicar to the eldest sister, 'have the goodness to tell me why you forbad the banns?'

'She is silly, and doesn't know what she is doing.'

'Do you mean,' asked the vicar, 'that she is of weak intellect, and not able to manage her own affairs?'

'Yes, and that she got our mother's property by unfair means, and now, if she is not stopped, she will throw every farthing of it away, and have to go to the union.'

'Bean't I allowed to speak, sir,' cried Nancy.

'No,' said the vicar. 'I cannot listen to you now. I do not know how far your sister is justified in attempting to stop your marriage,

but I will receive any statement she has to make
to me, and lay it before the bishop. Then
everything, you may be certain, will be settled
in proper order.'

'Come along, Nancy,' whispered Jasper,
'we shall get no good here, and I know how to
manage. Come along,' and half dragging and
half pushing the solid body of Nancy out of the
door, the whole party followed, much to the
relief of the clerk, who had expected an out-
break of temper as nearly inevitable. 'You had
better go out at the other door,' he suggested to
the sisters, who, having observed a little twitch
in the fingers of Nancy, which they knew meant
mischief, were happy to avail themselves of that
means of avoiding danger.

Jesse, with the younger portion of the congregation, took part in the general laugh which
had been called forth by the unusual display
they had witnessed ; but his imagination was far
from being carried away with it. Even while
he laughed, he was musing on the best means
he could adopt to increase the little knowledge
he had obtained from the sealed paper.

On the previous evening he had waited
patiently for his brother and sisters to satisfy
their curiosity, and then set himself to work, as
he said he would, to criticise it. He was a

rapid writer, and had quickly short notes of it in his pocket-book, with names of persons, villages, towns, and cities referred to by the writer, specially marked out for future use. On retiring to his room and looking over his notes, he could not restrain his satisfaction from breaking out into words, 'This is far better than anything I could get from Lea.'

I have the route he took marked clearly here, and if I set out upon the same lines, I cannot fail to meet with some persons who were acquainted with him, or to whom he applied for information. If his account is a true one, I may find the means of correcting his failure, and if it is not true on my return, I shall be in a position to force the truth from him through fear of punishment. Full of hope that he was at last upon the right track, he retired to rest. But he was a stranger to his usually unbroken sleep, and even his dreams assumed the character of his wakeful thoughts.

On returning from church after Nancy's exhibition was over, he took the opportunity of mentioning to his father the subject that was uppermost in his mind. He did not fully go into his project, but only so far as to show how anxious he was for a little change, and that he had a great wish to go to Germany and visit some of the places his mother was so much attached to, and which the brief narrative he read last night had brought so vividly before him.

'I think I perceive your object, Jesse,' said his father kindly ; 'but if you were to undertake the journey, it could only lead to disappointment.'

'I suppose it will prove rather an expensive trip ?'

'I was not thinking of the expense,' rejoined his father, 'but I will not at the moment say that I object to your going ; give me an hour or two to consider of what you wish to do, and I will then tell you what I think of it.'

'I trust your answer will be favourable.'

Sir Edward said no more, but retiring to his room, sat down alone and was soon lost in thought. More than once he rose from his chair and walked with a nervous step up and down the room. He could not quite understand his son. 'At one minute,' he thought, 'his love affair was of the most trifling character, and at the next he was disposed to think he was inclined to make it the business of his life. Though he does not speak plainly of his purpose in going, I am well assured that the parentage of the orphan children is its chief feature. And what will be the effect if he is successful ? Should he discover they came of beggars, would that cure him of his fancy ? or if he is unsuccessful, will he still think of Miss Montag, of whose history he must remain totally ignorant, as one he could ask me to receive as a daughter ? '

After mature consideration, looking at the unfortunate position in which he was placed, he arrived at the conclusion that the least chance of mischief lay in his sanctioning his son's visit to Germany. The variety of scenes through which he would pass, and the different characters he would come in contact with, he thought must have a good effect on his mind, and perhaps cause him to view his love affair in a very different light to what he then did.

And so in the silence of his own room the question was settled, and Jesse shortly afterwards, to his unbounded delight, was made acquainted with the fact.

' I shall not want to be away from you,' he said, ' for any length of time. I shall rapidly run through the country, and see and hear everything that is interesting to a mere traveller. I shall not go as a student to study men and

manners.   I want particularly to see some places
I have heard you speak of, where my mother
spent many happy days.'

'Will you take a servant with you,' asked
his father.

'No, unless you wish me to do so.   I think
I should feel more independent alone.   I do not
care to have a man constantly running about
after me.'

Little preparation was needed for the journey,
and little it had, so that when he set off the
next day his brother and sisters had scarcely
realised the fact of his going until they were
called upon to bid him farewell.

Scarcely had an hour elapsed from the time of
Jesse leaving the Hall, when a messenger arrived
with a letter from Mr Cresswell, begging Sir
Edward at once to come over to Downend to
see him.   'I am not very well, to-day,' he added
in a postscript, ' or I would have ridden over to
see you, instead of troubling you to come to me.'
Sir Edward did not hesitate about complying
with the request, but after having written a
note to a friend to put off an engagement he
had entered into with him for a meeting in the
afternoon, he mounted his horse and soon completed his little journey to Elston Court, where
he found Mr Cresswell suffering from a state of

nervous excitement, which he was vainly endeavouring to disguise from his wife and daughter.

'Come with me to my room,' he said to his visitor ; ' I have a little matter respecting which I wish to speak to you.'

As soon as they were alone, Mr Cresswell took a letter from his pocket, and handed it to Sir Edward with the simple remark of,—

' Please read, and tell me what you think about it.'

The letter was, as doubtless the reader has anticipated, from Lyson. It was written in a tone the very opposite to the one he had prepared to send before the return of Circum from his German business.

It would be difficult to find the proper name by which the epistle should be designated. In flattery, it exceeded the most fulsome expression that one could readily conceive. In humility, as from a beggar to a prince. In words of deep repentance the most sad and sorrowful, and but for one fatal fault, it would have been a perfect specimen of its kind—it was a little overdone. And that it was that had alarmed Mr Cresswell, and caused him to send to his friend to come to him, and that it was that caused the colour to come and go in the face of Sir Edward, as his eyes conveyed to his brain the full meaning of the words before him.

'Well,' observed Mr Cresswell as he received the letter back, 'do you understand it?'

'I am afraid I do too well,' was the reply. 'It appears to me to be but another attempt to work upon your feelings to procure a further supply from your purse to enable him to continue in his course of profligacy.'

'Yet,' said Mr Cresswell, 'there is something in this totally different from anything I have hitherto had from him.'

'Do you not discover in this the trace of another hand beside his own?' asked Sir Edward.

'I cannot say,' replied Mr Cresswell. 'He has placed me in a cruel position. If only the half he says of his repentance for his past misconduct to me and his wife is true, should I answer him harshly, and he should upon the instant, as he almost threatens to do, terminate his miserable existence, and the knowledge of the truth should reach the ears of Edith. I am fearful of the effect it would have upon her. I am afraid I should feel that she looked upon me as being little short of his murderer. But I am growing old,' he added with a sigh, 'and this may be but my fancy.'

'Why not let Edith see the letter and judge for herself?'

'It was upon that question,' replied Mr Cresswell, 'that I most desired to speak to you. What Edith's real feelings are towards him I can have no doubt. From the first year of their unhappy marriage, he has done nothing but what has been calculated to beget contempt. But she is, as you know, of a gentle, loving nature, and would, I believe, be very glad to see him reformed.'

'And place herself in his power again?'

'That I am not prepared to say,' replied Mr Cresswell, 'though if he could give lasting proof that his repentance was sincere, coupled with a determination with God's help to lead a new life, I think I could not advise her not to do so.'

'If you are not afraid to let her see the letter—'

'I am not afraid,' said Mr Cresswell, 'but I would rather keep it from her for the present.'

'And from her mother also?' asked Sir Edward.

'Yes,' replied Mr Cresswell; 'their knowledge of it would lead me at once to some decisive action, which I am anxious to avoid until I am better satisfied with the real condition of the writer's mind. You see,' he says, ' he has left Marseilles, and is now at Boulogne, where he awaits a letter from me to authorise his return to Downend.'

' Was your permission necessary for that ? '

' You remember the condition upon which he receives his quarterly remittances.'

' Oh yes, but I had for the moment forgotten it.'

' So far, then,' said Mr Cresswell ; his present application is in accordance with our agreement. Still, I am not satisfied that he is the changed man he represents himself to be. I want to ascertain the truth by the personal investigation of some one I can implicitly trust. The thought struck me when I sent my messenger to you, that if you could spare Jesse for a few days I would get him to run over to Boulogne, and act as my agent there.'

' I am sorry,' said Sir Edward, ' that I cannot oblige you in that, as Jesse has this morning left us for Germany.'

' You surprise me,' said Mr Cresswell. ' I had no idea that such an event was in contemplation.'

' Nor had I a few hours since,' rejoined Sir Edward.

He then related to his old friend the incidents of the last few days, and concluded by saying,—

'Perhaps you will think I have acted a little precipitantly, but I was sorely perplexed with my discovery, and I had almost decided to come over and consult you, but I thought I ought not to trouble you with it.'

'Do not talk of trouble,' said Mr Cresswell warmly, 'but rather of the pleasure I should have had in receiving you, and giving you my warmest sympathy and best advice.'

'You are very good,' said Sir Edward; 'but now to return to your trouble. Have you no one else to whom you could entrust your delicate mission? I would say, let Oliver go; only I am persuaded he would be unequal to the task.'

'I could send my solicitor,' said Mr Cresswell thoughtfully; 'he would need but little instruction to carry out my views. Or would it be more to the purpose, do you think, if I were to go myself, and discover with my own eyes the truth or falsehood of that which so nearly concerns the happiness of my daughter?'

'You are scarcely equal to the journey.'

'I certainly am but poorly to-day,' said Mr Cresswell, 'but with such an object in view, I think I could fortify myself for it.'

'As far as I can judge,' said Sir Edward, 'your idea of sending your solicitor appears to me to be the most reasonable plan you have touched upon.'

'Then he shall go,' rejoined Mr Cresswell in a tone of decision; 'I will send for him immediately. He is an active, clever man, and will not be easily deceived, nor hesitate to expose a sham, should one come before him.'

'And now, with respect to the ladies,' said Sir Edward, 'can you keep them in total ignorance of what is passing?'

'Not in total ignorance perhaps.'

'I think you will find that they must know all or nothing. If you could for the present keep the matter entirely from them, I would not argue the point with you; but if you cannot, the little they know will only increase their desire to know more, which will react in anxiety and worry upon you.'

'I am afraid you are right,' said Mr Cresswell.

'Come, then,' rejoined Sir Edward, 'let us put a bold face on the matter, and tell them unreservedly the whole truth as far as it has yet come before us; and if I may venture to go a little further, I would ask you to remember your oft-repeated promise to bring Mrs Cresswell and

Edith over to Woodfield to spend a few days with us at the Hall.'

'Since you are good enough to repose such entire confidence in me, incidents must for a time at least require that we should be much together. If you were stopping with me the necessity of our frequent journeyings from one to the other would be avoided, and with them, doubtless, much unprofitable excitement. My children will be pleased to welcome the ladies, and I will not attempt to tell you how much pleasure it will afford me once more to play the host to you.'

It needed but little argument to press the truth of all this upon the mind of Mr Cresswell, and to render him not only willing to accept the invitation, but to look forward to the visit with unfeigned pleasure.

In a short time they had arranged their mode of proceeding, and Mr Cresswell was in the drawing-room with his wife and daughter speaking openly of what he had before not dared to utter even in whispers.

CHAPTER XIII.

WITH unbounded pleasure the young people at Woodcome Hall received their visitors. The sudden departure of Jesse for Germany, the cause of which they could not understand, had made them a little restless and out of spirits, but that instantly passed off into the background on the introduction of their friends. Charlotte had so many inquiries to make respecting the parish work at Downend, and so many answers to give as to what they were doing in Woodfield, that the dulness of the last day or two passed unnoticed away.

Mrs Cresswell was charmed with the vivacity of Grace, who recounted to her many of the amusing things she had read of in books, and some which she had seen with her own eyes, amongst which stood out prominently the late exhibition at the parish church.

'Oh! I do wish,' she said, 'you could have seen Nancy and her companions; they were such comical figures that, when I saw them, I was obliged to cram my handkerchief into my mouth to keep me from laughing outright in the church.'

'I am glad you did not laugh there,' said Edith.

'But I did, only I kept the noise in my mouth with my handkerchief; and you would have laughed, too, I do believe, if you had been there. Why, I saw a smile even on papa's lips, and Charlotte's too, although she tried to look very serious. But Oliver and Jesse, they both sat down and covered their faces with their hands, and if papa and Charlotte had not been there we should all of us, I do believe, have laughed out altogether.'

'Then it was fortunate for you that papa and Charlotte were there,' observed Mrs Cresswell.

'And what is to be done now?' continued Grace. 'I am sure I do not know. I heard Charlotte say that Mr Gordon had written to the bishop; but Oliver can tell you better about that, as he was with Charlotte when the vicar told her.'

'I was talking to Miss Gordon, and did not hear what he said,' observed Oliver.

'Oh! you have begun to talk to the ladies, have you?' said Edith.

'Yes, a little,' replied Oliver, blushing scarlet.

While this was passing in the drawing-room, Sir Edward and Mr Cresswell were seated together in the library. The former busy reading and answering letters, and his companion leaning back in an easy-chair with the newspaper, which had escaped from his hands, lying on the floor.

This state of things had continued for some time, when Mr Cresswell, becoming conscious that he had been a little drowsy, readjusted his spectacles, which had gone awry on his nose, and taking up his paper, said,—

'Bless me, I do believe I was nearly asleep.'

'Indeed!' said Sir Edward, looking up from his writing. 'I hope the room is not too warm for you? I have nearly finished my task, and I shall soon be ready to take a stroll with you out in the open air.'

A very short time at Boulogne served to supply Mr Bevan, the solicitor, with all the information he required. He discovered Lyson at an hotel where gambling engaged no small portion of the time of the visitors, and saw him in the company of a class of men from whom most people are careful to keep at a distance.

He learnt from his own lips the state of his mind.

He was not instructed to make himself known to him or play the part of a spy upon his actions, further than to accomplish the objects of his mission, which was simply to discover whether the writer of the late letter was, or was not, the repentant sinner he represented himself to be. Having satisfied himself that he was not, Mr Bevan did not waste time to secure further evidence of the profligate's mode of life, but returned directly to London.

In his report to Mr Cresswell he summed up his opinion in a few words. He said, ' I believe Mr Lyson to be living in the very opposite way to that in which a stranger, after reading his letter, would expect to find him, and that his only object in writing to you as he did was to extort money to enable him to meet the demands which his mode of life is constantly pressing upon him.'

Mr Cresswell and Sir Edward were alone together when the report arrived. After having carefully studied and debated the question under its new aspect, they resolved simply to tell Mrs Cresswell and Edith that the solicitor had satisfied them that his investigation respecting the real character of Lyson had been most search-

ing, and had confirmed their worst fears, so
that for the future it would be well for them all
if they thought and talked of him as little as
possible. To Lyson Mr Cresswell wrote a
brief reply to his long letter. He told him
plainly that he had deceived his friends so many
times before that he could not now believe one
word he said, and therefore to talk of forgive-
ness with the view of receiving him again into
his house was quite out of the question.

But that as he had not broken his engagement by returning to England, his quarterly
stipend would still be paid to him as heretofore
at Marseilles. That it would be useless for him
to seek to have the place of payment changed,
as such a request under any circumstances
could not be complied with. That he had
chosen Marseilles himself, and there alone
would it be sent.

Mr Cresswell comforted himself with the idea
when he sent his letter off that that would put
an effectual stop to the importunities of his unworthy son-in-law. His wife and Edith seeing
the effects of this on his countenance, yielded
themselves willingly up to the conviction that
the measures he had taken would tend to their
general happiness. But bitter disappointment
lay in ambush ready to seize upon them and

banish their dream ; but as its shadow had not reached them, they strolled about the Hall and grounds in blissful ignorance of the threatened storm.

Strange coincidents are of daily occurrence in the world around us, which, if they were all recorded, the half of them would be set down as improbable or impossible. But that must not deter us from recording one that happened about this time in the progress of our story.

When Lyson left Marseilles he was accompanied by Circum, who, when they reached Boulogne, left his principal there while he crossed over to Folkestone. There, fortunately or unfortunately for the success of his diabolical scheme, he met with an old acquaintance who had just obtained possession of a large sum of money, which would probably set the telegraph at work and put the police on his track.

There was no time for explanation. ' I am off for Spain,' he said, ' by a vessel that leaves Boulogne to-night. Have your ears open, and if you hear of any inquiries for me, send the gentlemen to look for me in Holland ; and take that for your trouble. But bear in mind, if you betray me, you are a dead man ; I am not alone in this business.'

' Never fear,' said Circum, as he thrust the

handful of sovereigns he received into his pocket, and passed as unconcernedly away as if the transaction that had taken place between them was of the most ordinary character.

'This,' he thought, with a glow of satisfaction, 'will change the appearance of things. It will enable me to go on my own hook, and give me a better chance with Lyson. He is a very good fellow, take him altogether, but just a little too fond of himself, and pressing a man into his service for what he likes to give him.'

'Now, what is to be done? This does not appear to be a choice place for me to spend much time in, but I must stop here a day or two for the sake of the friend who has just left me. First, then, strengthen the inner man with a good dinner; next brush up my clothes, and get a new pair of boots; then get my beard and hair trimmed, and look out for any business that may come to hand.'

Whether he was able to turn aside the inquiries after his friend he did not know, but he spoke freely of the robbery that had been committed near Maidstone, the account of which he had read in the papers, and did his best indirectly to send the police off in the wrong direction; but that only in the way of common conversation with any one he chanced to speak to. He paid little attention to certain men who might be seen hanging about near the pier when a packet or sailing vessel was about to leave the harbour. He saw through their disguise; but as they did not speak to him, he did not feel himself called upon to volunteer any statement to them. So they looked carelessly at each other, and went on their separate way.

After spending three days at Folkestone, without any noticeable incident occurring to him, he walked up to the station, and having secured a ticket for London, entered a third-class carriage, and proceeded to make himself quite at home with his fellow passengers, the most of them being women.

Now comes one of the coincidents that so often happen in life, but which perchance some astute critic will say has been introduced here in order to help on our story to the end. Well, be it so; we will not stop to argue with you. But we may venture to say that if you had been in that carriage on your way to London on that particular day, you must have been dull indeed had you not marked the bright eyes of Circum just after the train left the Ashford Station, as he looked at a girl, or young woman rather, who sat by the side of a motherly old dame, who appeared to have charge of her.

Something in the young person's face had attracted his attention on the instant of his entering the carriage.

'She reminds me,' he thought, ' of some one I knew years since, but whom I cannot now remember.'

Smartened up as he had been by the barber, he was not a person a passenger would shrink from. Though he was evidently to all eyes an old man, his manners were youthful and pleasing. He appeared to have carefully attended to the growth and shape of his beard, which was perfectly white. A man who has lived on his wits till his seventieth year must have seen his best days if he could not suit his conversation to any company he would be likely to meet with in a third-class railway carriage, and, for aught we know to the contrary, in a first.

Circum had not been confined to one station in life. He had started from a point in the tree a good distance from the bottom, and had again and again run through the different branches from thence to the roots in the ground.

The brightness seen in his eyes after they left the Ashford Station was occasioned by his

having heard the name of Sir Edward Harewood pass between the old dame who sat on
the opposite seat and her daughter, or charge,
or whatever she might be.

On arriving at the different stations on their
way, changes were constantly taking place
amongst the passengers—some hurrying out
and some jumping in ; but amidst all the
changes Circum managed, without any seeming design, to keep as close to the two who
had specially engaged his attention as it was
possible for him to do. At Tunbridge he was
very polite to them, and during the ten minutes
they stopped there he brought out a cup of tea
for the old lady and a bun for the younger one,
they having previously been requested to take
care of his seat during his absence.

When the train was again in motion, if there
had been any ice between them it was then
fairly melted. Mrs Wilkins felt assured there
could be no harm in talking to such a polite old
gentleman. Had he been young, she would
perhaps have drawn her charge more closely
under her wing, and turned a scowling face
upon him. By the time they reached Chisle-
hurst they had begun to take quite a friendly
interest in each other. Mrs Wilkins learnt
that the very polite old gentleman before

her was from the Continent, and was going to London to see all the fine sights there. He had some little fear, he said, that he should find it very awkward, after his day of sight-seeing was over, when he sat down alone without a single soul to speak to of whom he had the slightest knowledge.

'If I could only get into some quiet family during my stay in the great city, it would add very much to my comfort and pleasure.'

'If I had a spare room,' said Mrs Wilkins, 'I should be proud to place it at your service.'

'Perhaps,' said Circum, 'you can recommend me to a friend. Most likely my stay will not exceed a week, but I should not mind paying a month in advance to secure a comfortable home. We could settle about the difference when I left.'

'We live at Islington,' said Mrs Wilkins, 'and that is a long way off from Cannon Street, where the train stops ; but if you would like to go with us, I think I know a neighbour who would be able to make you very comfortable.'

'A thousand thanks !' exclaimed Circum. 'I shall be delighted to avail myself of your kindness. You have not much luggage, I suppose, as you say you have only been from home for a couple of days, and I have but a

small bag ; so we can all go in one cab.   I
hate having a parcel of luggage to drag about
over the country with me.'

Cannon Street, the cab, and Islington followed in quick succession, and a neighbour's
door was soon open to Circum on consideration
of his paying for his rooms a month in advance.

And who was Mrs Wilkins, that had made
herself so useful to the traveller, who but the
old servant to whom Sir Edward Harewood had
entrusted Miss Montag, to keep her out of the
way of his son.   The visit to Folkestone arose
from the fact that Mrs Wilkins had a married
daughter living there, who had invited her to
spend a day or two with her.   She had received
instructions from Sir Edward to do the best
she could to amuse the girl, and keep her from
thinking too much of home, and she wisely or
unwisely thought that she could do nothing
more likely to answer his purpose than to take
her down to see her daughter.

Circum had now the coast clear before him.
He knew a great deal more than he did when
he left Folkestone, and he felt, to his great
satisfaction, that he was in a fair way of soon
knowing more.

By return of post Mr Cresswell received an
answer from Lyson, which had been prepared

by Circum before he left Marseilles, in anticipation that it would in the course of time be required. The tone of this second letter was even more submissive than the first. It went on to say how dreadfully grieved the writer was that his former application should have been received so unfavourably, but that, when he looked back upon his past life, he could not be surprised at it, as he knew how much he had offended his best friends by the thoughtless extravagance of his youth.

He then went on to say that he could not, however, rest without making one more appeal, as he had just heard from his sisters that his father was little better than in a dying state. He concluded his letter by saying,—

' Pray, excuse me for telling you I must come over and see him once more before his departure from all his worldly cares, of which my sisters write so pathetically, or I shall die here in a strange land from a broken heart.'

' The brute!' exclaimed Sir Edward on reading the letter. ' Has he no sense of shame, to arouse him to his abominable hypocrisy? But say what you will, under the pretence he has sheltered himself, you cannot prevent his visit to Downend. You may, however, avoid seeing him. You must not return to Elston Court while he is at the vicarage ; and there is but little fear of his venturing over here to see you.'

' I must put myself entirely under your guidance,' rejoined Mr Cresswell, ' as I am beginning to feel, I suppose from age, quite unequal to the tasks he so mercilessly thrusts upon me. You think he will cross over the Channel without any further correspondence between us ? '

' If he has not already crossed,' replied Sir Edward. ' I am prepared to think it will be but a question of a few hours. The letter, I think, shows his fixed determination to visit his father under the pretence of seeing him before he dies. What his ultimate object may be remains to be seen. I cannot tell you how very glad I am to know you are here with us.'

' Then, I suppose, we must consider ourselves your prisoners for an indefinite time ? ' said Mr Cresswell with a faint smile.

' Even so,' said Sir Edward ; ' but I trust you will not find your prison house very irksome, or its master a hard jailor.'

Sir Edward was right with respect to the conclusion he had arrived at concerning the movements of Lyson, for no sooner had that gentleman despatched his last letter to England than he prepared to follow it. His undertaking the journey had now become to him a matter of sheer necessity for his own personal comfort and safety.

His ill luck with cards and dice had followed him to Boulogne. With all his skill by day and night he could scarcely gain enough to say with a clear conscience that he was not on the losing side. His purse consequently, which was never, only by fits and starts, full, was now nearly empty, and although he had but little hope of replenishing it at his father's or sisters' expense, he knew if he could reach the vicarage a bed-room would be prepared for him, and that, while there, he would not want for the necessaries of life.

He had received from Circum a statement of his journey to London, and a brief account of certain discoveries he had made by the way, which he hoped shortly to turn to their mutual advantage. Before he left his hotel to go on board the packet, Lyson scribbled a few lines to his confederate, to let him know that he was about to set off for Downend, where he should expect to see him as soon as he could make it convenient to run down. He would not him-self call at Islington, in the first place, because he would be expected at the vicarage ; and in the second, he did not feel certain that he should find Circum at his lodgings even if he was at the expense and trouble of going there.

By this time Sir Edward was getting a little anxious about Jesse. He had heard from him on his arrival in Germany, and two or three times afterwards. His letters, however, which were at first lively and hopeful, soon became brief and cheerless. Up to the time of his last letter, he had made no discovery in the object of his search. He had been, he said, to several places mentioned by the old steward, but he could find no trace of him or the children of whom he was in search.

While in this state of suspense respecting the well-doing of Jesse, that the evenings might not hang heavily on their hands, Sir Edward made a point of inviting a few friends to join his little home company; amongst them not the least prominent figures were the vicar and his daughter, who were especially welcome to the young people of the Hall. Their entrance about this time was particularly looked eagerly forward to by Grace. Day by day she was hearing things of Nancy and her forthcoming wedding which greatly excited her imagination.

The gossips of the village had led her astray

on more than one occasion, and she had been
to the church to see the wedding only to find
the doors closed, and not a sound to be heard
within.　She had wearied Charlotte and Oliver
with her inquiries and suppositions without any
satisfactory result.　A little out of temper with
their apparent indifference, she had declared she
would not ask them another question about it,
but get her information direct from the vicar,
as of course he must know all about it better
than they did.　And of course he did ; but as he
did not wish to have any more display at the
church than was absolutely necessary, the first
intimation that Grace had of the marriage came
from a merry peal of bells, to let the world know
that the ceremony was over.

‘Oh, Mr Gordon,’ cried Grace as he entered
the room in the evening, ‘how could you be so
cruel as not to tell me that Nancy Dicks was
going to be married to-day ?’

‘There has been so much uncertainty respecting it,’ replied Mr Gordon, ‘that I was not quite
clear that it would take place here till the last
moment.’

‘Oh, do tell us all about it.　Was it very
funny ?’

‘The finish was worthy of the beginning, and
that you saw, I believe.’

'Yes, and I did so much wish to see the end. Now, do sit down and tell me all about it.'

'Perhaps your friends are not so much interested in the affair as you are,' said the vicar.

'Oh yes, they are, or they will be when they hear it,' cried Grace. She then ran round the room from one to another, saying, 'I know you would like to hear of the wonderful things that have been done, and you, and you, and all and every one. It must be so funny.'

By her energetic action she drew all eyes towards her, and her father, ever on the watch with his children to improve any incident that had the promise of innocent amusement in it, took his place by her side, and said he for one would be pleased to be very attentive, and listen to the wonderful account that the vicar had to give of the much-talked-of village marriage.

This encouragement was enough for Grace, and she at once took more active steps to force the vicar to do as she wished. She played the spoiled child to perfection. Dragging a chair to a vacant place in the room, she led the vicar to it, saying as she did so, 'There is a nice seat for you to sit down upon, and begin your story.'

'And where shall I begin?' asked the vicar.

'Oh, just after you left the vestry that Sunday morning.'

'Then I must at once,' said the vicar, 'go on to the following morning, when I received a visit from Nancy and, I hope, her now happy husband. She said she could not understand why I paid any attention to what her sisters said. In short, she wished to know why I did not order them out of the church. I told her I could not do otherwise than I did; that I would write to the bishop, and until I heard from him she must be patient, and not trouble me.

'"I don't want to trouble you, sir," she said abruptly, "but I do want to get married."

'"Come along, Nancy," I heard her companion say, "come along; I told you it would be of no use for us to come here. We must go to London or somewhere else and get a licence, that's the thing for us to work with." Saying which, with a "Good morning, sir," he unceremoniously drew her from the room.

'I must now introduce a little hearsay. I am told that, directly after leaving me, the marriage party set off for London, where they obtained the desired licence, and shortly afterwards made their way into a church and prepared themselves for the marriage rite. But the strangeness of their appearance and the

marked eagerness of the bride, caused the
curate, who happened to be present, to hesitate,
and then tell them he must speak to his rector
before he could go on with the service.

' " Oh, you are only what they call a curate, I
suppose ? " cried Nancy. " Well, I am glad we
found you out, for I mean to be married by a
real vicar. Come along, Jasper, and all of you,
we will go to another place. You see it is all
right, we have got the licence, and we will find
a vicar, and he must marry us."

' It is understood,' continued Mr Gordon,
' that they tried with no better success at two
other churches, and then determined to return
to the country and try at a neighbouring village.
It was then getting late in the afternoon, and
to add to their misfortune, the vicar was out,
and the curate, who had heard something of
their previous performance, would have nothing
to do with them.

' In due time I received an answer from the
bishop, to the intent that I must not refuse to
marry Nancy, unless a doctor would certify
that she was of unsound mind. That of course
the doctor could not do, and so after all the
business came back to me, and I had but little
time to wait when they knew I was ready to
receive them.'

' And they are really married ? ' said Grace.

' Yes, really,' repeated the vicar ; ' and I suppose we may now expect to see the carrier business of the village in a very flourishing state.'

' And had you a great crowd at the church ? '

' No; I believe they were in too great a hurry to answer my summons to bring many of the curious with them, and I had, as far as I could, kept the affair quiet.'

While the course of life was thus running on in England, Jesse was pursuing his solitary and unsatisfactory journey in Germany. For some days after his search had become hopeless, he tried to cheer himself with the idea that he should be more successful at his next halting-place, but he only reached it to have his disappointment repeated.

' I was a fool,' he thought, ' to leave home as I did. I was in much too great a hurry. I ought to have spoken to Lea, and learned from his mouth some further particulars of his statement. I knew the world was a place of change, but I did not dream of the footprints of Lea so soon passing away if he stopped at the hotels indicated in his statement; and as for the events spoken of by the gentlemen at Brighton, I cannot find even the shadow of their ever having taken place. I cannot have been in the right track for them, and the further I go the more doubtful I become of the truth of any part of Lea's statement. Poor Lizzie, I am afraid you will be sorely tried in your ignorance of where I am or what I am doing, and your trials will only increase when I return and you hear of my ill success.'

At length he was convinced of the utter use-lessness of going any further forward in the present state of his knowledge. Faint and weary he began to retrace his steps. He had fairly worn himself out in the eagerness of his pursuit. He had not been content to call at the hotels and villages, named in his notes, only, but he had turned aside to the right hand and to the left to make his search the more sure. At first his step was light and elastic, his eyes clear and bright with expectation, but all was changed now. His step was heavy and his eyes dull. He could not disguise the fact, even from himself, that he was becoming daily, nay hourly, less able to bear up against the fatigue of his journey.

On reaching Cologne he resolved to lie by quietly for a day or two in the hope of recover-ing his wonted energy. When he recommenced his journey he felt but little refreshed, and now another cause for anxiety pressed upon his mind. He had for some time, in the hope of having something to communicate of a pleasing character to his father, put off from day to day his letter. He now tried to perform his task, but in vain. He felt that he was not equal to a long letter, and to send a short one and say he was ill was not to be thought of. All that he could therefore do in his present unhappy position was to hurry home by the quickest route as soon as possible.

But the next day, on reaching Brussels, he was so ill that he could scarcely get out of the carriage that took him from the station to the hotel. The manager, seeing his weakness, led him into a room near the door, and asked him if he had not better have medical advice.

' Have you an English doctor near at hand ?' asked Jesse, as he sank down exhausted in an easy-chair.

' I think we have one in the hotel,' was the reply.

' Please ask him to come to me,' murmured Jesse, as he closed his eyes from very weariness.

Shortly a physician entered the room, and going up to his patient, who still sat motionless with his eyes closed, said in a soft, bland voice, ' A little overdone with a long journey.'

'Good God!' cried Jesse, 'that voice,' and springing to his feet he found standing before him one of the gentlemen he had met in the hotel at Brighton.

END OF VOL. II.

COLSTON AND SON, PRINTERS, EDINBURGH.